CASTLE CHANSANY

CHARLOTTE E. ENGLISH

ISBN: 9789492824240

CONTENTS

DRAGONSKIN

Sorting through Wizard Garstang's Potionery one airy, improbably-coloured bottle at a time, Jessamine went through what seemed an infinite number before happening upon the one she sought (and too many of these ended up splashed over the rosewood floor, alas, or would have, were it not for the ever-ready sylphs catching them up and sweeping them to safety before they could fall).

The chosen phial bore no obvious signs of difference from its fellows, Wizard Garstang being the meticulous type, and preferring the contents of his Potionery to match exactly. It was six inches tall like the rest, bulbous in the body and graceful about the neck, and tightly stoppered with some porous material ("So that they can breathe," Wizard Garstang had answered upon enquiry, without specifying who or what or how).

Jessamine knew this bottle (a clear glass, just faintly tinted with emerald) for the one she sought by the great eye that slowly opened within, blinked once

"

at her, and then slid sleepily closed. Emerald like the glass was this eye, only a thousand times more vivid, with a slit, black pupil. The wisdoms, glories and resentments of uncountable years glittered in the depths of that eye, and Jessamine was not sorry that it did not open again.

She put the bottle into her velvet potion-bag, and carefully tied the string. This she hung (securely!) from the belt of her mustard-yellow gown (a colour no one would have chosen, for its hue reeked of seedy magics and bile; but Jessamine was grateful for the luxury of the fabric, and she liked besides the way its skirt swirled over her hips).

'You have got it?' asked a gossamer voice, floating somewhere above her left ear.

'Safe and sound,' said Jessamine. 'As you have kept those I elsewise would have ruined. Stars! I swear the poxy things throw *themselves* off the shelves.'

'Why, but they do,' said the voice.

'I hope the Wizard pays you well for your service, then, or he'd have nothing of his Potionery left.' She wondered as she spoke what a sylph might want by way of currency, for their lives in Castle Chansany must be simpler than most of its residents. Did they wear clothes, or require sustenance? Jessamine had never seen a sylph, not possessing the requisite eyes, but she thought not.

'Does he pay *you* well,' said the sylph, 'to fetch his trinkets?'

'He pays me in knowledge,' said Jessamine gravely, for it was true, though her secret heart wished for some halcyon day when she might, against all odds, advance beyond the lowly status of Apprentice Potioner. Then might she not command fees of her

own? She could choose how she lived, and where —
and the colour (and fit) of her gown would be her
own to determine.

Frivolity to think it at all, and the Wizard, were he
to hear of it, would raise that terrible, satirical brow,
and send her at once to clean the Mixery. But
Jessamine, half a fairy and half a human, with all the
uglinesses of both, had no other beauties to enjoy.
Might she not, someday, aspire to a ribbon or two?

'They need not even be silk,' she said, thinking of
ribbons.

But the sylph thought still of knowledge. 'Do they,
then, craft books out of silk?' said the sylph, intrigued.
'I hadn't thought it so.'

'The Wizard would have such an oddity,' said
Jessamine. 'He has one of everything somewhere, I'm
sure of it.'

Including a sleeping and fearsome old power
stopped up in a bottle, on the topic of which, she
ought by now to be halfway to the Dispensary with it.

With a bob of a curtsey for the sylphs — it never
hurt to be polite, with ethereal things — Jessamine
hurried out of the glittering, colour-drenched
Potionery, closing the door upon its old oak shelves
and bottled secrets.

Her lithe little feet carried her post-haste down the
three passages that divided the Potionery from the
Dispensary, one hand cupped protectively around her
velvet potion-bag as she went.

Wizard Garstang sat ensconced in the best-of-all-
chairs, the thing having taken up a station in the
shadowiest corner of the Dispensary. It did not
belong in there, of course; there was scant room for
so oversized an article, and its jewel-coloured

upholstery and curlicued conceits were ill-matched with the scrubbed, dark wood of the walls and floors. But the chair, like most of Castle Chansany, obeyed the Wizard's bidding; where it was wanted, it was wont to appear.

The Wizard wore an embroidered surcoat and a velvet mantle, as befit his status. It wasn't called frivolity when a man wore finery, Jessamine knew; perhaps because there were no ribbons. The jewels adorning his fingers, and the curls to the toes of his shoes, didn't count.

Wizard Garstang's swarthy countenance lit with something upon seeing Jessamine; was it relief? 'Ah! You have it,' he said, leaping lightly out of his chair.

'Of course,' said Jessamine, a touch crossly, for did he have no faith in her at all? (Or in the sylphs, at any rate; she need not mention how many bottles they had saved from a messy demise). Untying the emerald-tinted bottle from her girdle, she offered it to the Wizard. He did not take it with his own hands, but instead wafted the phial aloft on a stray wisp of mist. The sleeper did not wake; all that stirred within was a low glimmer, as of a dying fire.

'There, shall that do?' said Wizard Garstang, but not to Jessamine. She had not seen the person into whose care he intended to consign the bottle; as far as her eyes could tell her, he was alone.

'Admirably,' said a hissing voice, and what had appeared to be a darkened sconce upon the wall writhed about, shedding its iron-wrought semblance and becoming a boggle. The boggle, pale as milk and a little greenish, but clad in fine Court attire, clambered down the wall and righted himself upon the floor; then, bowing to the Wizard, he plucked the proffered bottle from the air, pulled out the stopper with a swift, deft movement, and downed the contents in one swallow.

'But—!' said Jessamine, appalled, for *something* had been imprisoned within. Something alive.

The boggle looked at her. 'Treganda's daughter, are not you? My regards to your mother.' Then, after belching out a gout of emerald-coloured flame, he sauntered to the Dispensary door and out into the passage, leaving Jessamine staring after him.

'He didn't *pay*?' she said, in great indignation.

'Payment is coming,' said Wizard Garstang, with a look of unholy amusement. Jessamine knew that look. It meant the Wizard was up to something.

A suspicious glare, however, failed to elicit an explanation, and she knew better than to ask. The eyebrow would go up, his dark eyes would fix her with a gimlet glare, and he would instantly find more work for her to do.

'He knows my mother,' she said instead.

'I fail to see the relevance.'

'I hope you won't incinerate him completely, if he is a friend of hers.'

'Only a little bit? Would that be permissible?' Up went the eyebrow.

'About the edges, perhaps,' said Jessamine. She had not yet ceased to pity the sleeping creature with the unsettling eye, greedily gobbled down, as though it were a stomach-settling draught, or a headache remedy.

Wizard Garstang did not reply, nor did he move. He stood frozen, head lifted, as though awaiting something.

'He seemed awfully pleased about something,'

Jessamine suggested.

'He is to be disappointed,' said the Wizard.

A crashing sound split the silence, and the sudden roar of a ferocious inferno.

The Wizard began to smile, and then to grin; and when, moments later, the Dispensary-door opened again, and a thing of living flame wandered in, the grin became positively gleeful.

The flame-thing spat in disgust, spraying globs of white flame about the floor. 'Something tastier, I believe I said?' — uttered with the suppressed tumult of a forest fire, and laced with flaming crackle.

'You object to boggle?' said Wizard Garstang. 'But seasoned liberally with baseless arrogance! And, I believe, more than a hint of foolhardy ambition?'

'Succulent enough, I grant you,' said the fire-thing. Jessamine expected more, but it did not speak again. It looked up at the Wizard, licking its flaming jaws, and the bursts of fire wreathing its slender body, tapering tail and three, scaly legs dimmed a little.

Wizard Garstang permitted the emptied bottle to float to the dragon's feet, and with a further grumbled curse, uttered in syllables incomprehensible to Jessamine, it slithered over and poured itself down the neck, neatly bottling itself once more.

The emerald eye stared hard at Jessamine, in its depths lurking a twinkle of... satisfaction? Amusement?

Then the eye closed, and vanished.

'That dragon has only three legs,' said Jessamine after a while.

'The fourth was lost.'

'How?'

'I haven't asked.'

'I suppose it would be rude.'

'The wise are not rude to dragons, as a rule,' agreed the Wizard.

Jessamine only nodded.

'You are not going to ask me why I have fed your mother's friend to a dragon?'

'I should suppose he deserved it.'

'Perhaps it's only that Dragonfly was hungry, and I am a tyrant.'

'Naturally you are a tyrant,' said Jessamine. 'You're a *Wizard.*'

He smiled.

'Besides, he appears to have fed himself to the dragon.'

'So he did.'

'Expecting a different outcome, was he?'

'He imagined himself worthy of one.'

Having no further interest in the matter, Jessamine made him her graceless curtsey by way of farewell; it didn't hurt to be (passingly) polite to Wizards. 'I'll return Dragonfly, shall I?'

Wizard Garstang gave her back the bottle, this time with his own hands, which were warm and oddly roughened. *Hers* were so, and no wonder, with all the scrubbing she did; but what business had a grand Court Wizard with callused fingers? A puzzle, and Jessamine made the mistake of looking up, startled, into his face, as though the answer might be found there.

He was laughing at her. 'Carefully now, Jess-o'-mine. If you break Dragonfly's bottle, you will be the next delicacy in his banquet.'

Jessamine clutched the bottle close, thankful she had not run through the winding passages between the Potionery and the Dispensary. 'He wouldn't find me at all delectable. Perhaps one of the Court ladies, by preference.'

Wizard Garstang's glinting grin reappeared. 'I should like to feed every one of them to Dragonfly. Go,' he said, flicking his fingers towards the door. 'And *do* be careful.'

Outside, Jessamine found a display of scorch-marks streaking the cool stone some halfway down the passage. As she passed by, they shimmered silver, and melted away, leaving no trace of the boggle or his unhappy fate.

Save for one jewel: a small ruby, whose fire-licked depths offered some hint as to how it had survived the incineration of every other of the boggle's effects. Jessamine put it into her velvet potion-bag, next to Dragonfly's bottle, and went on to the Potionery.

A gale greeted her upon crossing the threshold — tore the hapless door out of her hands entirely, and sent it slamming wildly against the wall. A revolt in full swing, she quickly saw: the deep shelves, labelled in Wizard Garstang's own looping script, stood empty, their contents ferociously a-whirl above Jessamine's head.

'Shut the door!' called three airy voices at once, not so gently-wafting as before, now more of a howling cyclone in triplicate.

Jessamine tried, but the winds fought her, and she, small and spindly as she had always been, had not the strength to overcome them.

'You must shut the door!' she cried, and this command being more promptly attended to than she had expected, she took a vast leap back over the threshold and into the passage, just in time to save herself being brained by the flying door.

Two potions tore out after her. A common Toading Draught she caught in her quick hands before it had flown far; but the Wizard's signature mix, a Wishful Elixir, made it almost as far as the Mixery before she snatched it up. Feathery wings sprouted beneath her fingers, and she winced as the sharp pinions stabbed at her hands.

'Stop that,' she grumbled, squeezing both bottles as hard as she dared. It would not do to shatter the glass, but she *was* displeased. 'And so will the Wizard be, when he hears of this!' she admonished.

The Wishful Elixir quieted, its roil of colours fading to a dull, sulky grey.

She could not leave Dragonfly in the midst of such chaos. He would be shattered to bits in seconds, and then what? He appeared to like his bottle, having slithered back into it with apparent alacrity. What might a boggle-eating fire-licker do to a mere Jessamine, if she smashed his house?

All three potions found a place upon a high shelf in the Mixery, Dragonfly's bottle separated from the rest by a clear four feet, and the Mixery door firmly locked.

Later, standing with her arms elbow-deep in the stone sink of the Mixery-Room, scrubbing away the remains of a Purging Draught, Jessamine heard the one sound she had dreaded all morning through: a shattering and a splintering, as of glass rendered abruptly into dust.

'Stars alive, can a fairy not work in peace?' she roared, terror emerging as fury. The lingering vestiges of Purging-Draught went everywhere as she wrested her arms free of the muck, and tore across the room.

It was not Dragonfly's bottle: that fact alone could (to some degree) quiet her racing heart, and soothe her anger. The emerald-tinted phial stood, meek and quiet, at its separate end of the shelf, half-hidden in shadows and the draping lace of a cobweb.

Nor was it the Toading Draught, which sat like a mud-coloured rock at the other end, peacefully bubbling.

'Twas the Wishful,' sighed Jessamine. 'It would be, of course,' that being the next-most horrible possibility. The bottle lay in a thousand pieces, having shattered so heartily as to leave traces of itself sprayed all over the floor. The contents were grey no longer. Purple and periwinkle, turquoise and moss, and the strange, indeterminate colours of heartache: the myriad colours were racing down the shelf, pouring over the edge, and generally making another great mess which Jessamine would be obliged to dispose of.

Intent as she was upon this fresh calamity, only belatedly did Jessamine observe that the Wishful had run a long way down the long, oaken board, and before she could prevent it, the miserable stuff engulfed Dragonfly's bulbous little house.

'No—!' she started, hurling herself after it, but too late. All the colours merged into the emerald-tinted glass, which began to smell, unaccountably, of berry-pie.

'Drink me,' said Dragonfly.

Jessamine stopped. 'What?'

'*Drink me.*' It could only be Dragonfly speaking, what with the crackle of flames all in the words.

'I certainly shan't,' said Jessamine.

'Why not?'

'You'd devour me,' Jessamine said, folding her

arms, and backing a pace or two away from the compromised shelf. 'Burn me all up, like that foolish boggle. And what have I ever done to you to deserve it, I ask you?'

'Maybe I wouldn't,' whispered Dragonfly, oddly seductive. 'Maybe you would devour *me*.'

'I do not wish to!'

'I wish somebody would.' The voice was mournful now, almost weeping.

'You aren't making any sense,' said Jessamine, beginning to feel cross again. 'And I have cleaning to do.'

'*Drink me!*' roared Dragonfly. '*I command it!*'

'I answer only to the Wizard's commands,' said Jessamine, and with a sniff of disdain turned her back upon the too-colourful bottle and returned to the sink.

There followed a quantity of inarticulate snarling, and a sensation of intense heat against her skin. She did not turn again. If she did, she would witness Dragonfly, out of his house again, and trying with all his might to terrify her into obedience. And there was no saying but that he *might*, for a Jessamine was a small, weak thing, no match for fire-lickers.

When the snarling had quieted, she said, without turning her head: 'Perhaps if you were to explain, instead of roaring?'

'*Explain?*' spluttered Dragonfly.

'Why you would wish to be imbibed. It's a strange request, you must allow.'

After an indignant silence, which lasted a full minute at least, Dragonfly said: 'It's my Dragonskin.'

'Your… your *skin?*' Startled, she turned her head, and beheld a formless inferno occupying the darkest corner of the Mixery. 'Have you got any, under all that flame?'

'Yes,' said Dragonfly bitterly. 'And you don't want it, do you? No one does.'

Picturing the lifeless hide of a dragon, deprived of its innards, and draped all over the shelf, Jessamine was silent with horror.

'I thought the boggle might do,' said the dragon, heedless of the effect of his words. 'But it's no good. There wasn't enough of him.'

'Then why ask me?' Jessamine squeaked. 'I'm no taller!'

'What has height to do with anything?'

Jessamine began to answer, but finding herself incapable of a sensible response, gave up the point. What *had* height to do with anything, indeed? 'What is it I am to do with your Dragonskin, supposing there's enough of me?' she said instead.

'Why, wear it! What else would one do with it?'

The Wizard, she thought, would drape it over his best-of-all-chairs, and sit on it. Perhaps that was why Dragonfly had not plagued *him* with his peculiar request.

She asked anyway. 'Did the Wizard decline?'

'I haven't asked him, and I shan't,' said Dragonfly. 'What a preposterous dragon he'd make!'

True, reflected Jessamine. There had not been enough of the boggle to make even a halfway dragon (and upon reflection she could see that there was not; strange that it had escaped the Wizard), but there was far too much of Wizard Garstang. He would burst his bounds, like a swollen river, and his *Wizardliness* would go cascading all over.

Probably Jessamine would have to clean it up.

'So I'm to be dragoned, then?' said Jessamine. 'I am sorry, but I'm no clearer about the business than I was before. Why should you wish to give up your Dragonskin?'

'I am tired,' breathed Dragonfly, and the searing heat, mercifully, lessened. 'For all that I'm only a potion, I'm a potent one, and I've been much employed.'

How long the dragon-potion had lurked upon the shelves of the Potionery, Jessamine could hardly say. Certainly she had not seen him before, but she had been the Wizard's Apprentice for less than a year.

'You would not have to clean the Mixery,' Dragonfly said, and Jessamine stopped scrubbing, arrested.

'Or the Dispensary,' he went on. 'Or the Potionery, either.'

Jessamine dropped her scrubbing-brush. It fell into the soapy, grimy water with a splash, wetting her apron and, underneath it, her gown.

'I see I have your attention,' said the dragon.

'You do,' she allowed.

'Well then, let me see!' Restored, by hope, to high good humour, Dragonfly obligingly ceased to burn her at all. 'What else do you want? There is not much you could not have.'

'Living in a glass bottle, pouring myself down other people's guts all day?' Jessamine narrowed her eyes. 'You have funny notions of freedom, sir.'

'No, no! That isn't at all how it would be. What is it that you want?'

'A ribbon,' said Jessamine.

'A ribbon?'

'Silk, and the colour of the sky in summer.'

Dragonfly was silent a moment. 'Is that all?'

'Yes.'

'It can't be.'

'It is.'

He scoffed. 'I thought you a weightier sort of person.'

'Then there cannot be enough of me, can there? You had better ask someone else.' She resumed scrubbing.

Dragonfly, ruminating, did not answer. At length he said, slyly, 'When I was younger, I used to go all about the Castle. With the Wizard Baldringa. She did nothing but that she asked for my counsel.'

'I thought you said you were only a potion.'

'And you are only a girl.'

'You make an excellent point.'

'So you'll do it?' The flames erupted again, bright with hope.

'I'll *think* about it.' Jessamine returned to her scrubbing, and this time Dragonfly did not interrupt her.

After all, would it be so very bad if she failed, like the boggle, and became dragon-food? The Wizard would soon find someone else to clean his Mixery, and she had never excelled at the Wizardly arts herself. Even *he* agreed that she never would.

She was here only because of Mother. The fairy half of her heritage came from Treganda; a famous Court beauty some twenty years ago, Treganda was as ravishingly beautiful as she was difficult of temperament. Jessamine's utter failure to inherit either of these qualities had been an eternal source of disappointment to Treganda (who did not imagine herself difficult so much as charmingly wilful); so when the Wizard Garstang, somewhat the worse (or the better) for the Queen's honey wine, had offered her an Intolerable Insult, and subsequently a forfeit in recompense, the beauty had been quick to demand an apprenticeship for her gawky, impossible child. The fact that Jessamine had neither aptitude for nor interest in Wizardry had been nothing to her.

Why the Wizard had agreed to such a forfeit in the first place, or kept her on afterwards, remained a source of mystification to Jessamine.

As did the nature of the Intolerable Insult, which neither Treganda nor the Wizard would ever tell her.

She'd stayed because she recognised in her mother's manoeuvrings a desire to be rid of her obligations to so strange a child; and being fed and clothed in the service of so magnificent a character as the Court Wizard rather beat scrubbing pots in the scullery.

An alternative future for her daughter as the resident Court Dragon might please Treganda just as much. And there was considerable beauty about Dragonfly. It was not the beauty of silken wings and tresses, like her mother's, nor that of velvet gowns and ribbons, such as she craved in her secret heart. It was the beauty of strange and ancient magics, of elements and nature and power and myth, and Jessamine gave the possibility serious thought — at least until she had finished cleaning the Mixery.

'Well?' rasped Dragonfly from his bottle, as she staggered back over the threshold with her burden of buckets and mops.

'I am sorry, Dragonfly, but I believe I cannot,' she said, setting the buckets down for a moment. 'You see, you make a strong case for Dragonhood, but that isn't what I am. I am a creature of four plain limbs and shivering in the winter, and I don't know how to be a dragon.'

'You would soon learn,' said Dragonfly.

'As I have learned Wizardry?' Jessamine, shaking her head, picked up her buckets. 'I'm afraid I would be poor at it.'

'How do you know, if you haven't tried?'

This question, being unanswerable, went unanswered. Jessamine left the Mixery, taking the Toading Draught with her, but leaving Dragonfly behind.

'Have you been cleaning again?'

Wizard Garstang, having rung for his third-favourite spell-book to be brought into his study at once, regarded Jessamine with a frown as she came trotting in.

Jessamine, startled, looked down at herself. Had she splattered her gown with Purging Draught and soapsuds, and failed to notice? Or perhaps that mischievous Wishful had got onto her as well as onto Dragonfly.

She saw nothing but mustard-coloured cloth, only slightly wrinkled, and her own unlovely body beneath.

'The Mixery was very dirty,' she said defensively, and set the third-favourite spell-book — less weighty than the first and second, and relatively sober in appearance, a mere dark clothbound tome with silver etchings — onto the low table at his elbow. He was in his best-of-all-chairs again, the thing installed in its regular place before the stone hearth, and somehow contriving to emit a steady reading-light.

'I have other people for that,' he said, making no move to pick up the third-favourite. 'Will you not *use* the Mixery?'

'I thought you liked me to clean, being as you're quick enough to send me for the scrubbing-brushes.'

'Only when I am trying to annoy you, Jess-o'-mine. I can see I shall have to try a different approach.' He picked up the third-favourite at last, and made some show of leafing through it, but Jessamine did not think his mind was on the spells.

'It amuses you to annoy me?'

He subjected her idle question to more depth of thought than she had expected, and after some moments of rumination announced: 'It does not precisely amuse me, but I hope someday it will benefit me.'

'Benefit you?' Jessamine eyed him with sour disgust. 'I can't see how it could.'

His grin appeared, and a gleam of exactly the amusement she had accused him of. 'No, but I'm persuaded you will. What happened in the Potionery this afternoon?'

'I don't know. The Potions took it into their heads to hold a riot.'

'Again?' His brows went up — *both* of them, this time. 'Why, they haven't done that since Year's Turn.'

'I can't think what set them off.' Jessamine made a move to retreat, navigating carefully between an enormous jarful of twinkling butterflies and a precarious stack of cloth-and-leather-bound tomes towering up from the floor.

'I imagine it was Dragonfly, for some motive of his own. He's restless just at present.'

Jessamine frowned. Her mouth wanted to speak,

to tell him about Dragonfly's odd request, and find out his opinion of it. It half-opened, all ready to pour forth the words, but some other instinct shut it again.

'Yes?' said Wizard Garstang, observing this aborted attempt.

'Why is he restless?' she said.

'Dragonfly? Oh, he has a fit of discontent about once a year, and sleeps much of the rest of the time. They say he was an excellent Familiar to one of my predecessors, but that must have been a long time ago.' He bent his head over the third-favourite, and began to read.

A Familiar! Jessamine had always heard that Wizards had Familiars, but *her* Wizard had not seemed to; she'd thought herself mistaken. Was Dragonfly his Familiar?

'Why, he is as bad at it as I am!' she blurted, not making much sense; she'd meant he made as poor a Familiar to the Wizard as she made an Apprentice, and what a pity.

'That being so,' said the Wizard, without looking up, 'I fear our arrangement is to come to an end, for I have taken a new Apprentice. He begins in the morning. I am sure you will show him around the Mixery and the Potionery and so on, before you leave?'

Jessamine stood, transfixed with shock. 'L-leave?'

'Tambul will need your room.'

'B-but—' stuttered Jessamine. 'Where will I go?'

He looked up at last, and directed at her a dark, keen look, as though deeply interested, all of a sudden, in the subject of his erstwhile apprentice. 'Where would you like to go, Jess-o'-mine?'

'I wouldn't like to go anywhere at all!'

'No? Surely there is somewhere that interests you?'

She was silent. To be sure, there might be some other post in Castle Chansany she could take; even were it the scullery, it would be better than nothing.

But he had asked about her *interests*. The world beyond the Castle was large enough. Surely something of it might fascinate her?

'I like it here,' she said. 'With you.'

His eyes were smiling, she was sure of it, though his face remained grave. 'A solution will no doubt present itself by morning,' he declared. 'Do go away now. I simply must finish this cantrip.'

Jessamine, heart-stricken, turned in silence to leave.

'Do not even *think* of cleaning the Potionery,' he called after her.

Jessamine slipped silently out into the passage, and didn't answer.

The potion seared her throat a little as it went down. In its wake it left a burning sensation, more pleasant than otherwise, like the time Jessamine had finished the dregs of one of the Wizard's discarded goblets.

'I could have been the best-of-all-familiars,' she said sadly, 'If only he'd asked.' She dissolved as she spoke, her limbs turning to mist and then smoke and then flame. She waited to disappear, as the boggle had done; down into the innards of Dragonfly, never to be seen again. But she didn't.

'Wizards are no good at asking,' said Dragonfly. 'Not in any of the right words.' His name now made sense to her; he had the wings for it, once stripped of his Dragonskin. He was handsome, too, even if he was hundreds of years old. Perhaps he wouldn't get any older, now.

'I'd stay away from Treganda, if I were you,' she told him with a sniff, wreathing her smokish form around his lithe limbs.

Dragonfly shuddered. 'You do burn, you know,' he said, extricating himself. 'You'll have to watch that.'

'Sorry,' said Jessamine, too busy for remorse; it had struck her that she would never be cold again. Neither cold, nor frail, and the next time Wizard Garstang raised his left brow at her, and said something about the Mixery sink, she'd have exactly the means to annoy him.

No. She would have no opportunity to annoy him, for was she not to leave? She'd decided that herself, just before the potion had gone sliding down her throat. A Dragon need not remain anywhere she did not choose, and she'd have her house with her.

'How does it feel?' said Dragonfly, having stretched out his fairy-limbs ten times over, and turned a somersault that sent him right up to the ceiling. 'Shall you be all right?'

'I shall be the best-of-all-Jessamines,' she told him firmly. 'I can feel it already.'

He grinned, reminding her, for a moment, of the Wizard. 'We thought you'd be perfect,' he said. 'Take care of the Dragonskin. It's the first-favourite, you know.'

'Wait!' said Jessamine. 'Who's *we*?' But he was already gone, vanished out of the meagre window of her little Apprentice's room like a wisp of smoke his own self.

Grumbling, grousing and spitting flame, Jessamine made her way down to the Wizard's study, and slithered her way very carefully between the books. *You do burn, you know.* She had better watch for that.

He was still there, in his chair, with the third-favourite spell-book open on his lap.

'You could not have just asked, I suppose?' she said, taking care not to bathe him in flame. Or not too much, anyway.

He waved her fires away with a flick of his fingers, and set aside the book. 'I did ask,' he said.

'You didn't. I am sure I'd have recalled it.'

'I asked when I gave you the Dragonfly.'

'You did no such thing. I took it out of the Potionery myself.'

'And why did you do that?' The left brow went up.

'Because you wanted him for a customer.'

'In a manner of speaking. I thought a snack might appease the dragon, and that boggle always was an unpleasant fellow.' Garstang blinked. 'Whatever was his name.'

Jessamine, having never known it, could not assist him. 'Dragonfly was the customer?' she spat.

'One might rather consider the boggle as payment for services rendered.'

Jessamine's flames roiled in tune with her dismay.

'I shouldn't waste your sympathies upon him, if I were you,' said the Wizard. 'He was perfectly aware of the risk.'

'But what if there'd been enough of him? You would have got him for a Familiar! I can't think he would have been better than Dragonfly.'

'I thought it of all things most unlikely,' said the Wizard, unruffled.

'What if there hadn't been enough of me? I'd have been dragon-lunch.'

Wizard Garstang looked straight into Jessamine's fiery eyes, and the lurking smile was back in his own. 'You've always been enough, Jess-o'-mine. There wasn't the smallest danger.'

She sniffed, though the tip of her shimmering tail found its way to his wrist, and coiled loosely about it. 'I *am* magnificent, am I not?'

'Beyond anything.'

'Did you complete your cantrip?'

'I can make no sense of it at all. Will you take a look?'

Jessamine draped herself over the back of the best-of-all-chairs, and rested her snout upon her Wizard's shoulder. 'Open it up, then,' she ordered, and the Wizard retrieved the third-favourite, and offered it for his Familiar's perusal.

'I shan't be fed any boggles,' she said, suddenly suspicious.

The Wizard smiled. 'You shall have anything you wish, Jess-o'-mine. You're a dragon now.'

'A ribbon, please,' she said promptly. 'Sky-blue.'

But the Wizard made no move to produce one. He only turned his head, and looked up at her, waiting.

'Oh,' said Jessamine.

It was not a Wizard's power, the magic that stirred in her fiery depths. It was older, deeper, and stranger than that, and Jessamine needed only a thread of it.

'Delightful,' said the Wizard Garstang, with his glinting smile.

Jessamine, decked in ribbons and flame, purred her satisfaction. 'Well, Wizard,' she said, tapping the open pages of the third-favourite spell-book with the tip of her tail. 'About the cantrip.'

THE BEST OF ALL CHAIRS

When the dragon Jessamine slithered into the Wizard Garstang's study in the dark of the night, and undulated her way towards the best-of-all-chairs that skulked in a corner, a voice from the shadows took her by surprise.

'I would not sit there, if I were you,' said the voice.

While disembodied and confusing as to source, it could not be termed alarming; not even though the hour was late, and the night dark and silent. The words emerged too sleepily for that, as though the speaker were at least half asleep.

Jessamine paused. She had not known the sylphs to frequent the study very often, for the Wizard's caprice irritated them, and theirs had the same effect on him. But they were wise in the ways of Castle Chansany, and when they spoke, Jessamine listened.

From a distance of a safe three or four feet, Jessamine inspected the chair.

Nothing so personal to the Wizard Garstang could be modest, either in proportion or design, and so the best-of-all-chairs elevated the concept of *splendid* to new and dazzling dimensions. The tall, engraved back rose to a height of six feet; the seat was wide enough across to fit at least two people side-by-side; and the arms were of proportions eminently suited to the king's own throne. Moreover, while the greater part of an old oak tree had already gone into its construction, in the creation of its spectacular frame, the Wizard had desired that the thing should be soft as well. Hence the profusion of cushions, in hues of emerald and sapphire and gold; above all, the best-of-all-chairs advertised itself as *expensive*.

'Perhaps you think I will damage it, and displease the Wizard,' said Jessamine. 'And were it likely that I should, you would be right to prevent me. But my fires are my own, and shan't do anything unseemly to the chair.'

'The Wizard would never harm his Familiar,' said the shadowed voice. 'However clumsy she had been. But no, that was not my concern.'

Jessamine thought again. 'Perhaps what stands before me is not the best-of-all-chairs at all, but something else in a clever disguise.' She let her tongue unspool, and tasted a leg. The flavour, woodsy and old and dry, did not encourage a second taste.

'Like as not to be, with the Wizard around,' agreed the voice. 'But no, that was not my concern either.'

'Well then, what is it?' said Jessamine, abandoning so unsatisfactory a pursuit. 'I am tired, and I want to sit down. On something *soft.*'

'The Chair is in no mood for company,' came the answer, sleepily, and then nothing.

'No mood?' muttered Jessamine. 'What else does a Chair desire but to be sat upon, I should like to know?'

Nobody answered her, or not right away. A swishing sound came instead, and then into the pool of light cast by Jessamine's own wreathing fires there appeared: a carpet.

It was the thickest one, nicely rounded about the edges, and coloured like forest-moss.

'Aren't you supposed to be in front of the hearth?' said Jessamine, recognising it.

'I went for a perambulation,' said the carpet, settling itself in its accustomed place with a silky *sigh*.

'Refreshing.'

'Occasionally.' The carpet, to all appearances, went to sleep.

Jessamine nudged it with her snout, and when it did not rouse, she delicately bit the corner.

'You are rude,' said the carpet.

'I am,' said Jessamine. 'And since that is the case, I shall not hesitate to make use of the best-of-all-chairs, whatever its mood.' So saying, she flowed fierily up onto the broad, cushioned seat of Wizard Garstang's own chair, and curled up.

Nothing untoward happened. But, just as she was dropping into a comfortable doze, someone said lugubriously: 'I like that.'

Jessamine stirred. 'What's that?'

'Personal Chair to the Court Wizard,' the mournful voice continued. 'Every expense lavished upon me. And then I am made over to an *Apprentice*.'

'But I am not an Apprentice,' said Jessamine. 'Not *now*. I'm the Familiar.'

'You aren't the Wizard,' said the best-of-all-chairs. 'It amounts to the same thing.'

'I should suppose the Wizard to be asleep,' said

Jessamine. 'Or perhaps carousing.' She closed her eyes again.

'His fancy's caught,' said the chair. 'His eyes turned another way, and what is to become of *me*, I ask you?'

Jessamine pondered this. 'I think not,' she said. 'He was always more scornful than otherwise, when it comes to the Court ladies.'

The carpet intervened. 'Child, the chair talks of furniture.'

Jessamine sat up. 'The Wizard's got another chair?'

'A gift,' mourned the best-of-all-chairs (or, as Jessamine now supposed, the second-best-of-all-chairs). 'From the Queen.'

'Why would Queen Mellany give the Wizard a chair?'

'It…' The second-best-of-all-chairs paused, struggling in the grip of some deep emotion. 'It *flies*,' it managed at last, and fell into a brooding silence.

'Cannot you fly?' Jessamine enquired. 'I have seen you taking up the best of spots all over the Castle.'

'Not as such,' mourned the chair. 'Not like *that*.'

'Right.' Jessamine slithered off the chair. 'I've got to see this.'

Jessamine would have felt no surprise if the whole tale were to prove itself nothing but hocus-pocus. What the Queen would want with the Wizard such that she would give him a flying chair, well, Jessamine could not imagine. Surely the Queen was too busy ruling the kingdom with the King; what time had she to waste on frivolities such as unusually airborne furniture?

But when at last she discovered the Wizard (he having proved absent from his bedchamber), she found that the second-best-of-all-chairs was right.

The Wizard *did* have a new chair. What's more, the gossamer fairy-wings sprouting from its four graceful legs, and the top of its tall and elegant back, suggested that the tales of its powers had not been exaggerated.

And that the Wizard was enchanted with it could not admit of a doubt, for he was sleeping in it.

He made no attractive picture, sprawled all over the seat, with his legs thrown carelessly over one spindly arm (this chair not having the robust stoutness of the other), and his head gracelessly lolling. Jessamine supposed him to have been engaged in study of this new marvel, with his customary carelessness of time and tiredness, until he fell asleep where he sat.

His sapphire velvet mantle was sadly wrinkled.

Jessamine woke him with a waft of cinder-scented air.

He stirred, grunted something unflattering, and fell back into slumber.

'Wizard,' Jessamine hissed. '*Wizard.*'

His dark eyes opened, and fixed, unseeing, upon Jessamine.

'You make a spectacle of yourself,' she hissed.

Being Wizard Garstang, he had not fallen asleep in one of the many dusty corners of the Castle, a quiet, out-of-the-way place where no curious eyes could fix upon him. Being Wizard Garstang, it would not have occurred to him to take his prize into some such unobjectionable spot, and conduct his investigations *there*. No, not even though he *had* an excellent chamber of his own invitingly titled "Study".

The Queen had presented him with his new, splendid chair in the midst of Their Majesties'

Feasting Chamber, Jessamine knew, for that was where the Wizard had remained. And having fallen asleep, had acquired (or perhaps retained) an audience of: two fascinated Court ladies in moon-coloured silks; a Bard's apprentice, the callow youth trailing a lute and a green mantle much too big for him; a rival Wizard from a neighbouring kingdom, judging from the spangled garments he wore; and a pot-boy crept out of the kitchens to see the spectacle, not entirely hidden behind the golden brocade skirts of a banqueting-table laden with sumptuous delights.

Wizard Garstang took in all this in bemused silence.

'He wakes!' cried one of the Court ladies, following this enlightening comment with a peal of silvery mirth.

'We hope your repose has refreshed you, Wizard,' said her companion, more gravely.

'Yes,' said Wizard Garstang, and sprang out of his seat with one of his abrupt, effervescent bursts of energy. A pair of dancers, failing to foresee this possibility, almost collided with him; the Wizard's satirical brow rose as he watched them whirl away again, scowling. He did not offer the ladies so much as another syllable, but bent over his new chair, and became absorbed again in its various contours.

'He will be looking for evil enchantments,' said the rival Wizard, loftily, to the same ladies. 'It is what any Wizard does, upon receiving a new Wonder into his care.'

Jessamine's Wizard did not favour this with any response at all; deeming it beneath his notice, no doubt.

'No such thing,' said Jessamine firmly, and set the

rival Wizard's toe on fire with a lick of her tongue. 'The Queen would not give him anything evil.'

The rival Wizard was not long inconvenienced by his flaming footwear, for he smothered Jessamine's promising little blaze with an irritable gesture of his long fingers. The contemplation of the black burn now marring the beauty of his satin slippers distracted him, however, and he did not reply.

'What *are* you doing?' said Jessamine, turning back to *her* Wizard (for he might be every bit as self-satisfied, know-it-all and tyrannical as this other one, but at least he was *hers*).

Wizard Garstang, absorbed, did not reply.

'You have broken your best chair's heart,' Jessamine persevered. 'And it's my belief the furniture will be plotting a mutiny.'

'No, no,' he murmured, running a gentle hand along the edge of one silken, fluttering chair-wing. 'The carpet will keep them in order.'

'The carpet's asleep.'

'Well, and what else would you expect a carpet to do at this hour?'

Jessamine sighed, and slithered under the table, from which sulking-spot she emitted a fine flow of rose-scented smoke.

'I say,' came the Wizard's voice, 'You aren't too attached to these, are you?'

Jessamine peeked under the hem of the brocade table-clothes. The Wizard was chatting with the new best-of-all-chairs, and he had his fingers around the gossamer wings.

'Flying's awfully dangerous,' he continued. 'A high wind and ill-luck and you'll be dashed to pieces against some turret, or fallen into the lake. Care to trade?'

Whatever the chair said in reply, Jessamine could not hear. A soft-spoken thing, by appearances; nothing like the deep rumble of the best— no, the *second*-best-of-all-chairs.

Jessamine hoped its response was favourable, however, for in another moment, the Wizard said: 'Excellent!' and, with alacrity, plucked the glorious wings from the chair's high back. He bent, and a few swift gestures secured those adorning its four legs as well. He piled them all onto the seat, picked up the chair (severed wings and all), and made off with it.

Jessamine scuttled out from under the table, and ran in hasty pursuit.

Wizard Garstang pushed his way through the throng of the Queen's Feasting-Chamber, and once out into the passageways kept up a long, rapid stride all the way back to his study. A word, once fairly through the door, set all the sconces aglow, and the furniture woke up with a start.

The Wizard was no sluggard, when properly inspired. 'There,' he said, a moment later, stepping back to admire his handiwork. 'No ill effect, I think?'

The gossamer wings, taken from the Queen's gift, now fluttered gaily from the back of his erstwhile favourite chair — its back now extra tall and straight with pride, Jessamine judged. The four smaller wings sprouted jauntily from its thick, heavy legs.

The best-of-all-chairs, now restored to all the glory of the position, gambolled.

'Not yet, not yet,' said the Wizard. 'Not till we get outside.'

The best-of-all-chairs subsided.

'They do not match,' sniffed Jessamine.

The Wizard surveyed his chair. 'You are right,' he decided. 'What do you think? Ruby?'

'No! Horrible!'

'You're right,' said the Wizard again. 'Silver.'

'Nothing will do for *you* but gold,' said Jessamine.

She expected the Satirical Brow, in response to this sally. Instead, she received the Glinting Smile. 'Perfect,' he decided, and the wings turned a shimmering and stately gold.

Jessamine slunk up the legs of the Queen's chair (divested of its wings, and waiting hopefully nearby). 'This is my chair,' she announced.

Wizard Garstang's head came up. 'Ah. Yes. Just a moment.' Quite what he did, Jessamine could not tell; she knew only that a surge of magic swept over the chair (smelling, unpleasantly, of wet mud), and as it passed it left behind it an article of furniture much altered.

'Oh,' spake the carpet, softly. 'That's nice, that.'

Jessamine dug her claws into the blanket of soft (and really, scarcely damp) moss that now grew upon the seat of her chair, and stuck her nose into the nearest of the canopy of rose-blooms that hung from the back. The wood itself was no longer a pale deadness of hard edges and turned corners; now it grew in knots and whorls, like a tree again, only chair-shaped. 'Charming,' said she, with rare sincerity. 'Just needs one more thing.'

'The sylphs will see to the watering,' said Wizard Garstang, with a careless wave of his hand.

But Jessamine mustered her own blazing magics (a little musty with disuse, but functional enough), and manifested a spray of ribbons winding jauntily up each leg.

'Those don't match,' said Wizard Garstang, which was true enough, for a living tree-chair had no use for a set of woven fabric adornments.

'Yes, yes they do,' said Jessamine, and went to sleep in her chair.

THE FAR-BELOW

The Object – whatever it was – rapidly disappeared into the impenetrable, milk-white mists surrounding the walls of Castle Chansany. Jessamine listened in vain for the sound of its eventual impact, far below. *Far* below.

An awful silence followed this event, lasting some time.

Jessamine broke it at last.

'Something's fallen over the side.'

Saying it aloud made the terrible truth feel all the more real, and Jessamine's sinuous tail began an uncontrollable twitching. Weren't there supposed to be wards, and such? Invisible but infallible enchantments swaddling the sky-high castle in a comforting shroud of safety? Winds of magic! Currents of gramarye! Nothing was *ever* supposed to go over the side.

And Jessamine had not even the first idea what it had been. She'd strolled out to the balcony to take the air, puffing an amusing stream of perfumed smoke from her delicate nostrils; paused to enjoy the aesthetic delights of the rainbow-coloured forest flowers, rambling from pot to pot, and sprawling languorously along the silver fences; and then – and *then* – it had happened. An Object, small and fast-moving, had gone hurtling down.

She might have sworn, in fact, that the thing had hurled itself off the balcony, and into thin air.

Nobody spoke. She was alone out here, then, not even a sylph wafting about upon the dulcet breezes; hmph. No one to talk the matter over with.

Also, no witnesses.

Jessamine curled up at the base of one ornate, glinting fence and shut her eyes a moment, pondering. If no one had perceived the event save for herself, was it necessary to make anything of it?

Perhaps she hadn't even seen it. Perhaps it hadn't happened at all.

Her draconic lips stretched in a blissful smile, and for some three or four minutes she dozed in the golden sun, comforted by these charming ideas.

But, no. It wouldn't do. Something *had* gone over – something that glittered oddly in the sunlight – and if one didn't put a stop to such behaviour, well, who knew what might go over next? It might be one of the flower-pots, so pretty with their cerulean glaze. It might be somebody's hair comb all over jewels, and the Royal Court wouldn't stand for *that*.

It might be… it might be the first-favourite spell book, and *then* she'd be for it.

Jessamine's eyes snapped open in horror, all thought of slumber gone. Something had to be done. Not a doubt of it.

'I suppose,' she gulped, 'I'll have to fetch the

Wizard.'

Her ensuing trek through the castle was of the lengthy character guaranteed to leave her out of breath and patience both; but finally, *eventually*, she ran across the Wizard Garstang – near enough literally. He sat cross-legged upon the floor, his velvet-clad behind parked upon a curlicued rug, and tucked behind an ornate screen in a corner of somebody's bedchamber. Jessamine hadn't the faintest notion *whose*. He sat alone, but the profusion of silver coffee-pots scattered about him, together with far too many cups, saucers and silver spoons, strongly implied he had recently enjoyed company. Rather a lot of it.

'Wizard,' puffed Jessamine, her lashing tail toppling a hapless coffee-pot or two. 'You're needed at the Edge.'

'The Edge,' repeated the Wizard. Being face-down in a near-empty pot at that moment, deeply inhaling the dregs of whatever had once occupied it, he took no note of Jessamine's state whatsoever. 'Which Edge, my dear dragon, and why?'

'The Hindmost South-Western Balcony,' she snapped. '*That* Edge, and you're wanted because something's Gone Over.'

That brought him out of the depths of his pot; he raised his head, and blinked his dark eyes several times. Full of steam, she thought, or some such. Perfume. One never knew, with the Wizard. 'Gone Over? Gone Over where?'

'Gone Over *down*.'

'What was it?'

'How should I know? Twas a blur of something glitterish, and then gone.'

'You didn't throw it, did you?'

Jessamine began to swell with indignation, but before she had more than half doubled in size, the Wizard grinned, and said, 'I had to ask, Jess-o-mine, did I not? Admit it, you're in just the mood to engage in a spot of target practice.'

'Were your head the goal, mayhap,' she conceded.

'Quite,' said the Wizard, accepting this with admirable grace. 'But it wasn't you.'

''Twas not me. I was sunning myself, peaceful as you like, and there it was gone.'

At last, something like disquiet entered the Wizard's expression. He sat for a moment in thought, tapping a coffee-stained finger against one lip. 'Well,' he said, rising abruptly to his feet, and towering over Jessamine. 'Then something ought to be done, oughtn't it?'

The balcony was just as Jessamine had left it – flourishing with verdure, and empty of company. The Wizard spent some little time with his folded arms resting atop the balcony fence and gazing into the far-below.

Jessamine peeked, too, balanced atop the fence with her long tail wrapped tightly around the bars to steady her. There was not much to be seen for all the white clouds in the way, but perhaps the Wizard's eyes saw more than Jessamine could.

'There appears to be a hole,' he said after a while.

Jessamine looked, but saw nothing of the sort, and said so.

'A hole in the veil,' he clarified, with a trace of impatience. 'The veil, which is *there*, I might add, precisely to catch such things as would otherwise tumble down.'

'Or people,' put in Jessamine.

'Those as well.'

'And how did it get there?'

'The hole? Someone must be tinkering with my arrangements.'

He uttered this in tones of grave displeasure, which one couldn't wonder at.

'What then do we do?' said Jessamine. 'I suppose we must find this person.'

'I suppose we'll have to go down,' said the Wizard instead. 'After all, until we know what the object *was* it is useless to try to guess who wanted it.'

'You think it was a stolen thing?'

'I don't see what other use there would be in making holes in my lovely veil.'

Someone at Castle Chansany was a thief. The notion shocked Jessamine a fair bit, for the Castle did not receive newcomers often, nor did very many people leave; most of those as were in residence were *always* in residence, and how could any of them be so disobliging as to steal from someone else? Her tail began a staccato twitching at its tip, a fair sign of her anger, and since the result was a wobbling and a near-toppling from the balcony fence, she hastily got down. After all, there was a hole in the veil.

'You'll mend the hole?' she said, for the Wizard had put out a hand to steady her, and why would he have done that if he wasn't afraid for her possible demise? He was the forgetful sort, likely to hare off in search of the culprit and leave the problem unremedied.

'In due time,' he said.

'Ah,' said Jessamine. Well, that was that, then. 'So

it's down for you.'

'For us, Jess-o-mine. I'll want my Familiar with me. Our culprit and our object both might be down there, after all.'

'Me to go down,' said the dragon with a smoky sigh. 'But it's far-below.'

'You've wings.'

'And little practice at using them.' Jessamine had not been a dragon for long; only scant weeks ago she'd been a half-fae, with two legs only, and not a wing to her name.

'Here, then, is an excellent opportunity.'

Jessamine muttered something, stretched the fiery wings in question, and beat them back and forth. Air moved, but nothing much else. Certainly not Jessamine. 'They're too weak,' she announced. 'They'll never hold me.'

The Wizard's only answer to this was a gust of air – *cold* air – which swirled about Jessamine's clawed feet and wafted her into the sky. He himself had already summoned his favourite chair – the best-of-all-chairs. The thing came swooping in on its gossamer wings, and caught the Wizard up in its velvet-cushioned seat. The pair hovered, and so did Jessamine.

'Tarry a moment,' said she, flailing. 'I tell you, I cannot fly.'

'You must imagine better, my dragon,' said the Wizard gaily, and soared away. Some last few words came drifting back with the winds of his passage. 'The feat is only a thought away!'

Only a thought, and the thoughts passing through Jessamine's mind were not, at that moment, of the sort suited to a public airing. She growled, and spat a little flame over the edge.

It winked out of life in mid-air, smothered to death by all that nothing.

'Well, and so shall I be,' said Jessamine with resignation, and chucked herself over the side.

She had a fair view of the Castle from this inverted posture, and ample time, as she plummeted down, to admire all the beauties rapidly dwindling in size. Those turrets really were *lovely*, all the glass twinkling in the sun so– a frantic flurry of her smoky wings failed altogether to slow her descent– pity she'd not had another of Chef's butter cakes for breakfast, she *could* have, but she'd thought of her girth and refrained, *fool,* for what use had a dragon for a svelte frame if her wings didn't work and she was to be squashed flat in the far-below anyway?

An impact came, sooner than expected; it *hurt*, knocked all the breath out of her in a *whoosh*, but it wasn't the squashing kind of an experience; another breath came.

She'd shut her fiery eyes when she thought of Chef's butter-cakes. She opened them, and saw the Wizard.

'Tsk, dragon,' said he, smiling at her. He'd caught her as she fell, doubtless with a fancy flourish of his Wizarded chair, and she was saved.

'Not so much for flying, these,' she croaked, wafting smoke.

'Since that's so, you might stop flapping them about,' said the Wizard with a cough. 'I'd sooner breathe air than smoke.'

Jessamine, frightened into unwonted obedience, stopped. By the time she'd caught her own breath, and calmed the shaking in her limbs, the Wizard had brought the-best-of-all-chairs to a swooping halt upon some blessedly firm ground, and Jessamine was able to alight from her seat.

The far-below turned out to be leafy in character, and not much else.

'There's a forest here,' said she in surprise.

'Well, of course there is,' said the Wizard, striding off. The-best-of-all-chairs gambolled along after him, far more delighted than either of its passengers at this unscheduled outing. 'What else should there be in the far-below, pray?'

Jessamine had often peeped over the side, but had never glimpsed aught but wafts of clouds and mist; she'd dreamed up many a fanciful thing that may lie beneath, but the Wizard– he'd had the misfortune of *knowing*.

Now Jessamine knew, too, and a few airy dreams slipped away in consequence.

She sighed.

Still, it was more forest than she'd ever seen before, and interest revived. She had no names to put to the trees she saw, but they were vanishingly tall, and broad about their sleek brown trunks. Boughs reached out a long, long way, decked in all that extravagant greenery, and there was emerald-coloured moss up and down them, and all over the floor. She saw ferns, too – these she did know, for some of the Court Ladies liked to keep them in pots, and there were some upon the balconies.

'I'd like a fern,' she announced.

The Wizard was Questing. She knew it from the purposeful stride, and the set to the jaw, not to mention the rapt look in his eyes. But he answered her from some disengaged part of his great Wizard's brain: 'Then you'll have the best of all ferns, Jess-o-mine, but first help me find the Object.'

Yes. The Object. Distracted by all this far-below splendour, Jessamine had forgotten the purpose of the Quest altogether. The Object! Whatever it was had fallen right through the clouds and must have ended up amongst the ferns and the moss, but how were they to find it? Twas a small Object, and a large far-below.

She said this.

'Am I not a Wizard?' answered he. 'And do I not have a Familiar at my elbow?'

Jessamine, being farther away than that, scurried to catch up. He and the Chair were fairly off, trampling ferns aplenty in their haste; Jessamine flitted along behind, unsure what, as Familiar, she was to do.

'There's a cantrip,' said the Wizard. 'Scribed upon the eighteenth page in the volume of thirteen seasons past–' (He meant the second favourite spell book, Jessamine knew that one). 'It is for finding a lost *thing*, and now that I think of it, I ought perhaps to have brought the book with me.'

Jessamine gave a smoky sigh, curling the delicate leaves of a few passing ferns. 'Besides, how are we to use a cantrip on a thing when we've no notion of its identity?' She was looking all around as she scuttled along, her bright eyes on the watch for anything that looked out of place; anything that was patently *not* part of this verdant and squelchy far-below; but she could spend a year at the task and catch not a whiff of it, she knew.

'We must find assistance,' declared the Wizard, after a moment's thought.

'From the second-favourite book?' Jessamine had

a vision of the thing, called from far away, and hastening to obey its master's summons; hurling itself over the side, as she had done, and plummeting down.

'No, I have not the book with me. Did I not say that?'

'Then where's this assistance to come from?' said Jessamine. 'For we're all alone, if you haven't noticed.' Not so much as a rustle of leaves had she heard, save those she and the Wizard made themselves. Not even any brisk, scurrying creatures among the undergrowth were there, for with the clamour they were making they'd frightened the lot away.

But the Wizard looked Up.

'Ah,' said Jessamine, espying something feathered, and with a long tail. It wafted along the winds, far above, glimmering blue and red in the dulcet sunlight. She thought it would come down, convinced, in her befuddled way, that all about must obey the Wizard's summons as she did.

But the bird did not come down.

'There,' said the Wizard presently, not deigning to point.

Jessamine glimpsed it, perhaps. A flicker of green, but then there was so *much* green; how was she to tell one sort from the other? 'Something moss-coloured,' she hazarded. 'But up far too high.'

'Here it comes.' The Wizard waited, holding himself unusually still. Rare for the man to adjust his *own* behaviour to suit another's needs; he was trying not to scare the scrap of a creature, decked in wing, that came wafting slowly down.

'Twas a dragon, gathered Jessamine, and couldn't speak for shock.

At least, not for a moment or two. '*Well,*' she spat, curiously affronted. 'If 'twas a dragon you wanted, had you not dragons in sufficient number?' It wasn't even an impressive specimen, being far smaller than Jessamine herself, and all skin and bone. A youngling, barely out of the egg.

'But this one flies,' said the Wizard Garstang, with a smirk at his Familiar.

Jessamine might have sulked, save that the Wizard's expressions were becoming known to her. She detected, beneath the smirk, a conspiratorial smile. Something of fellowship, in this invitation to share a joke, though it came at her expense, and she settled down. Perhaps he was not fixing to replace her with this delicate thing, at that.

The newcomer frisked in delight, under the Wizard's gaze. She would soon be cured of *that*, thought Jessamine sourly, and condescended to sniff the creature, politely enough. It smelled of loam and sap and a whiff of petrichor, not unpleasant.

The Wizard spoke gently to it. It was only a baby, Jessamine reminded herself. It warranted gentleness, even if she didn't. 'Tell me, my tiny fellow. Have you seen an Object lately fall from the heavens?' And he pointed upwards, quite as though the dragon might comprehend.

It didn't. Jessamine read this in its behaviour, perfectly unchanged, say the Wizard what he would. It gambolled, it coquetted for attention – shameless thing – and it made a curious sound, *mrrrr*, and chirped. Someday it might grow larger, and develop, with all its new bulk, an intellect, and perhaps even an identity. Until then, it could hardly be worth talking to—

'Perfect,' said the Wizard, beaming. 'What a fine fellow you are.' He fed it something, Jessamine could not determine *what*, though it smelled sharp, and savoury.

'What,' said she. 'And have you derived meaning from this nonsense?'

'Haven't you? I must say I'm surprised.' The Wizard attempted, with a wave of his bejewelled fingers, to dismiss the dragon. The little creature proved impervious to suggestion.

'You fed it,' observed Jessamine. 'A mistake, that.'

'Well, then you shall have a companion,' decided the Wizard. 'He'll be a fine creature once grown, though perhaps too big for the Castle–'

'Tell me what it said,' interrupted Jessamine, impatient with this vision.

'Something fell,' answered he, in tones of surprise, as though this ought to have been obvious. 'We knew that, of course. But now we have some idea as to *where*.' As if these words had themselves proved a spur, he was off, swooping away in his Wizarded chair.

Jessamine scuttled along in his wake. If she fluttered her wings hard enough, they proved effective to boost her speed, even if not to lift her aloft; she made full use of them, and barely kept up.

The interloper, scarcely inconvenienced by the Wizard's pace, fluttered along too.

'Where are we going?' she called after her master.

'What I truly asked,' carolled he, 'is whether anything fell *that did not belong*, and our little friend has seen only one Object that he could not recognise. It glittered sharply, and caught the sun, and it fell somewhere in this direction.'

Jessamine, growing short of breath, paused, and took in the extent of the damp forest before her. Reams and reams of it, with no end in sight, and all frondy besides. 'Absurd, absurd,' cried she. 'Do you seek to stumble over it, in all this fernery? It'll never happen. We shall be here until Year's End.'

'I don't, at all,' said the Wizard agreeably, slowing. 'But *you*, perhaps—'

'Oh,' said Jessamine, for there it was, lying quietly at her feet. Such an innocent thing, inert among the moss, for all the world as though it had *not* led her and the Wizard a merry dance all the way from the Castle.

'There,' said the Wizard, with vast satisfaction. 'You always had a lucky way about you, Jess-o-mine.'

This being too patently absurd for words, Jessamine ignored it.

'Well, then, and what is it?' The Wizard came swooping back, the wings of his chair stirring the drooping ferns.

'It is a spoon.'

Wizard Garstang halted before this felled treasure, and regarded it in silence.

In point of fact, the spoon was bright silver, recently polished. A fine, wrought thing, fit for nobles to use at table, though in size it seemed more suited to the tea-tray.

Or possibly, the coffee-pot.

Jessamine's mind wandered back a ways, to where she'd found the Wizard. Reposed upon the floor, surrounded by a decimated collection of beverages – and a quantity of spoons.

'It is *your* spoon,' she accused.

The Wizard did not answer.

'It is just like all the others you had about you,' she persisted.

'Nonsense,' said the Wizard, briskly. 'The Castle must be full of such articles.'

'Doubtless,' Jessamine agreed. 'But how would one of *those* come to fall down into the far-below?'

'Well, and how do you imagine a spoon of *mine* should have done so?' He was growing testy, the scowl building upon his brow.

Jessamine, recognising the signs, persevered. 'Because you threw it.'

He scoffed, and coughed, and spluttered something incomprehensible.

'Perhaps you were in a temper,' said she, serene. 'Or perhaps you were showing off, for I doubt me not that there were ladies present. Was it not so?'

The Wizard, unusually, was silent.

'If anybody *else* were to throw a thing with sufficient force to hurl it over the side, its descent should, in all likelihood, be prevented by your Wizardly veil.' Jessamine, becoming smug, permitted herself a snicker. 'But if *you* were to throw it, Wizard-mine, how different a story. There's a fine hole burned in your veil, I'll be bound, and a long afternoon's work ahead to mend it.'

The Wizard bent, and collected the spoon. He examined it briefly, and then tucked it away into a pocket in his velvet coat. 'Tell no one of this, Jess-o-mine.'

'I might, perhaps, be encouraged to hold my peace,' she conceded. 'If I were to be suitably recompensed.'

The Wizard Garstang sighed. 'Shall it be comfits again? I'll speak to the kitchen.'

'Comfits aplenty,' said Jessamine sternly. 'And two or three butter-cakes.'

The Wizard eyed her. 'You could ask more.'

'But I shan't, for I'm a reasonable dragon.'

'And are you to assist me in mending this hole I've burned in the veil?'

Jessamine gave the matter due consideration. 'No, I shouldn't think so,' she decided. 'For the sun is not yet gone, and I've a nap to finish.'

THE QUEEN'S PHILTRE

Have you ever been to Castle Chansany?

Perhaps you go there as a pedlar, selling ribbons and cosmetics and jewels to the inhabitants of the Royal Court.

Perhaps you are a cook, or an ostler, or an apothecary, tending to the residents' many and varied needs in exchange for a few silvers for your own.

You may be a Wizard or a Wizard's Apprentice, oft to be found in the Libraries in the small hours of the morning, weary-eyed in pursuit of an elusive cantrip.

Or perhaps, just perhaps, you are a noble yourself, attending the Court in your satins and silks and making your bow to Their Majesties.

Have you, then, met the Queen?

Queen Mellany, they say, is a lady of surpassing handsomeness (if not, precisely, beauty). Doubtless her velvets and her jewels would grant handsomeness enough, even were she insufficient in feature. An air of majesty and power would supply the rest, would it not? And a queen must have a surfeit of both.

She is a little younger than His Majesty the King, but not much, with honey-coloured hair not at all given to grey (so they say). Her eyes are the colour of amethysts, proclaim the fanciful (or the fawning). Others speak of her voice, low and mellow, melodious as a lady's voice should be.

Perhaps these observers have seen her from afar, in Their Majesties' Feasting Chamber, or at a Royal Ball. They cannot have seen her in person, not up close. Not in the intimate fashion of a friend or an associate.

For if they *had*, they would sing a different tune.

If *you* have ever chanced to glimpse Queen Mellany in private — as she sits, almost unattended, in her glass-house, say, or before she retires to her bed — you might not speak of handsomeness or velvets, or of jewel-coloured eyes.

You might be more disposed to say: Her Majesty is *tired*.

'Fetch me the Wizard Garstang,' said this lady one eventide. She spoke in the dusty, whispering tones of profound exhaustion, so faint the syllables that one must strain to catch them at all.

But her lady-in-waiting (Aramanta, today) had sharp ears. 'Yes, your majesty,' answered she, and left the glass-house at once in a flurry of emerald silks.

The queen was left alone, which seemed to suit her, for she sat motionless, her eyes half-closed. There is at least one advantage to weariness: there is a peace in it, for if one has not the vitality to go rushing about the world, one must by necessity place oneself somewhere comfortable, and stay.

A deep serenity enveloped the glass-house once

Aramanta was gone, for everything else in it was passing into slumber. The sun's blinding rays were gone, dipped below the horizon, leaving a tranquil blue haze in their wake. The queen's flowers had furled their petals and stood dreaming in the dusk. Even the winged things that occupied the upper reaches of the rambling vines were silent in their nests.

A luna moth drifted slowly by, its silvered wings glinting in the moon-coloured light of the queen's crystalline lamps.

The night wore on and turned into morning, and the Wizard Garstang did not appear.

There came, though, another voice. A dry, smoky cough stirred the air near the queen's knees, and then somebody spoke. 'Majesty?'

Queen Mellany's eyes opened. They appeared a faded blue, barely any colour left to them at all, but perhaps it was a mere trick of the light.

A dragon crouched by her feet, the proud, ruby-shimmering head dipped in a show of respect (or possibly uncertainty).

'Yes?' said the queen, still in those dusty tones, for there was no need to exert herself *here*.

'What manner of service is it you want?' said the dragon, curling a long, fire-tipped tail around clawed feet. Something in the voice told Her Majesty that this creature was of a female persuasion, and she was looking expectant.

The queen achieved a frown. 'I am not acquainted with any red dragons,' she said, slowly. 'And I do not recall that I asked for one.'

'I wasn't either,' said the dragon in answer to this first observation. 'Until recently, when I turned into one. But I am not always red, as it happens. I was blue yesterday, and perhaps I shall be golden tomorrow.'

The frown deepened.

'And you did not summon me,' continued the dragon, helpfully. 'You called for my master Garstang, but being as he's the Wizard, well, he's nowhere to be found. They're rarely anywhere you want them, Wizards, and if they are it's like to be a week late.'

Queen Mellany said nothing, but the befuddlement creeping into her pallid face said enough.

'I'm Jessamine,' said the dragon. 'I was the Wizard's apprentice, once, though I cannot say as I was any good at it. I'm the Wizard's Familiar now, though, and I *am* good at that. Were you wanting anything a Wizard's Familiar might be able to do?' This last question was uttered with a note of anxiety, as though the creature were uncertain of her own relevance to the situation.

Her Majesty, however, had not the first idea. 'I need a new Philtre,' she said. 'The Wizard Garstang enchants them for me, and he must do so again, at once.' It took the poor lady some time to utter so many words together, but Jessamine did not lack for patience. She waited, politely enough, until the queen's words had ceased.

'It'll not be the classic sort of Philtre you're wanting, will it?' Jessamine mused. 'You've the love of his majesty the King already, not to mention a castle full of courtiers and a kingdom full of subjects. That's enough love for anybody, I should think.'

'Indeed,' said the queen.

Jessamine subjected her liege-lady to a long look

and a deep scrutiny. 'Something along the restorative lines, then?' she offered.

'Indeed,' said the queen.

'Hm.' Jessamine, perceiving that Queen Mellany lacked either knowledge of the subject or the capacity to express it, asked no further questions.

'If the Wizard's anywhere to be found, he'll be along soon, I make no doubt,' she said. 'But that's as may be. The matter's urgent, I judge.' She performed a fleeting bow, a dip of her rubescent head all wreathed in smoke, and grinned. All her long, pearly teeth showed. 'I will see what I can do,' she promised, and scuttled off.

The queen, bemused, said nothing, but slipped back into her half-slumber.

Queen Mellany was a merry figure, Jessamine would previously have said; merry and formidable in equal measure, a fair bit of each. A distant being of bright gold hair, a flashing smile, and an air of majesty only a born queen possesses.

But not today, alone in her glass-house, without her pomp and her ceremony. Without her Court. For a moment, Jessamine had felt the larger of the two, and she being but a small heart and a shrinking soul herself.

Which was the true queen?

The Wizard would know, but the Wizard was not to be found.

Jessamine scurried through the winding labyrinth of the Castle, barely aware of the passages she slithered down and the chambers she passed by. Her mind (small it may be, but it was keen, for all that) occupied her with reflections of a new kind: who among her acquaintance was all that they seemed to be? The Wizard, for instance. What might lie behind the vibrant, glittering colours of the man? Was he, too, a poor quailing thing beneath the arrogance and the laughter, like Jessamine? Or wearied to his very soul, like the queen, and only pretending otherwise?

The thought prompted a snicker. Inconceivable.

The door to the Potionery stood shut fast, with the impregnable demeanour of a locked and bolted barrier. A muffled clattering emanated from within, and a curse or two in Tambul's hoarse voice.

Jessamine made of herself a puff of smoke, and wafted underneath.

'What's amiss?' said she, reshaping her draconic curves upon the other side.

Tambul, the Wizard's new apprentice, turned an aggravated face upon her. His hair, never very well-behaved at the best of times, appeared to be staging a full-scale revolt, for every white wisp of it stood on end. His compact form bristled with indignation; the little man fair radiated rage.

'You look like to fly into pieces in another minute,' said Jessamine. 'Can you not mellow yourself a trifle?'

'It's those *sylphs*,' he spat, staring wildly at the empty air around him. 'They've taken the Wizard's Wishful Elixir, and I have but *just* finished Mixing it. He'll not be pleased, and then who'll be to blame?' He swiped uselessly at the air, coming up with nothing.

Jessamine, seeing nothing resembling a floating phial, judged the thing long concealed. 'Come, now, is this the truth?' she called. 'It is too bad of you.'

A chorus of laughter answered her, and then the phial reappeared. It was one of the larger ones,

Jessamine saw, airy glass, and filled to the brim with a parti-coloured liquid. Tambul had made a lot. 'But he is no *fun*,' breathed a voice in her air, even as the phial floated its way (sulkily) into Tambul's reaching hands.

'Aye, but you make him still less so with such treatment,' Jessamine reproved. She could not disagree with their judgement; she hadn't taken to the new apprentice herself, he being of a sour disposition, and not seeming sensible of his immense good fortune in assisting the Wizard Garstang. But he had talents far exceeding her own, this she could not deny, and the Wizard seemed contented with him.

She received only a gusty sigh in response. Tambul snatched up his phial and stuffed it immediately into the velvet potion-bag hanging from his belt. 'This'll not come out again until it goes into the Wizard's own hands,' he informed the air, scowling.

'Tambul,' said Jessamine.

The look he gave her might be irritable, but no more, the return of his Elixir having mollified him a shade. 'Yes?'

'We've an emergency.'

That word, to Jessamine's surprise, operated powerfully upon the Wizard's apprentice. He snapped to attention, forgot his grievances in an instant, and seemed somehow taller for it. 'What's the matter?'

'It's Her Majesty, the Queen, though not as I ever saw her before. She looks like to fade away any minute, Tambul, so tired as she is. I'd swear she was a century old, and never mind the golden hair. She wants a Philtre from the Wizard, but can't say as what's in it, and no one can find him.'

Tambul attended closely to this jumbled recital, and did not plague her with questions. 'The Queen's

Philtre,' he mused. 'Seems to me as I've heard mention of it before, but I've no notion how it's made. And we have nothing of *that* sort in the Potionery just now.'

Jessamine's heart sank. 'Then do you know where the Wizard has gone?'

His brows quirked. 'If the Familiar hasn't a notion, how then should I?'

Jessamine, flattened, gave a wispy sigh. When had anybody kept pace with the Wizard Garstang, after all? Not even *he* could keep up with himself, she'd wager. Things fell out of his brain as rapidly as they wandered into it.

'Then what are we to do?' said she. 'Where did you hear of the Philtre, Tambul? Did the Wizard mention it to you?'

'No,' said he, wiping his hands on the colour-stained apron he wore, before tearing it off. 'I've not been set to make any such thing. Twas in a book, methinks—'

'One of the grimoires?' interrupted Jessamine, her heart rising.

'Aye, but I'm forbidden to go into them except in the Wizard's own presence. *You* ought to recall that.'

'I do,' Jessamine agreed. 'So you would be. But *I* am not. I'm the Familiar these days, and he hasn't said as I'm to leave them alone *now*.'

'He hasn't *said* as much,' repeated Tambul. 'But does that mean he hasn't intended it?'

'It hardly matters,' Jessamine decided. 'We've need of those grimoires, and if the Wizard's unhappy with me he may tell me all about it later. For now, we're to the secret library, and quickly.'

The Wizard's study seemed a lively place, when the Wizard was in it. Not so much when it stood empty. It *echoed* in rather chilly fashion — an oddity, given the profusion of carpets and cushions and curtains; and it only did it when Garstang was off someplace, as though his absence had disembowelled it of something.

The-best-of-all-chairs stood in its customary spot in the best corner, towering over the more mundane articles of furniture, and sporting all the best of the soft things. It didn't speak as Jessamine and Tambul came in.

Neither did anything else, in fact, until Jessamine lightly kicked the mossy carpet that lay before the empty hearth. '*Whissht*,' uttered the carpet, a sound not unlike a sneeze. It quivered. 'Well, what is it?'

'Is the Wizard handy?' said Jessamine, to start.

'I've no notion at all.'

Not, then. 'Well, and is the Library about?' she tried next.

The carpet fluttered, a helpless little gesture. 'You'd have to ask the shelves.'

The Library should not, strictly speaking, be its own entity at all, being as it was a collection of shelves itself — and books, of course, always those. But things about the Wizard had a way of turning *odd*, and in this case, the Library had a will of its own.

Jessamine turned to the shelves, at least those she could perceive. Not part of the Library, these, or not officially; they were the ones that hung about in the open, where just anybody could see them, and housed only the lesser books. But if you wanted to find a Library, a bookshelf was always a good place to begin.

Jessamine redirected her question to these humble

creatures, wrought all of polished, dark wood as they were, and burdened with weighty tomes and bejewelled things. They occupied the wall several feet above her head, a lofty position, from which they loomed over everything except the-best-of-all-chairs.

A silence followed, rather a long one.

At length, a dusty voice said: 'And what would you with the Library?'

'I need a grimoire,' said Jessamine, promptly and firmly. If you sounded like you were uncertain of your right to things, people tended to get obstructive ideas. 'The Queen's in trouble, and the Wizard has the answer, and I've to find it. Quickly.'

'Righto,' said the shelf, and the wall behind it shivered. It had no right to perform so delicate a manoeuvre, being, probably, a foot thick and made of solid stone. It did, however, and it creaked as well, and *groaned*, and then — stopped, and fell silent.

Nothing had moved, not even the wall, and Jessamine experienced a profound confusion — until it occurred to her that all was changed. The shelf she'd spoken with was gone, perhaps, or only altered — hard to say, when everything was made from the same deep-brown wood and held a similar array of leather-bound spell books. But these were different books, and that was a different shelf.

'Oh, splendid!' she cried, and swarmed up the Wizard's favourite chair. The back of it rose quite six feet high, a suitable vantage-point from which a dragon (and but a small dragon, at that) might peruse the spoils.

Tambul stood upon the chair's seat. He would be made into gloves, Jessamine reflected, if the Wizard came back and saw him at it, but that was his own look-out.

Besides, they had a queen to save, and heroes were obliged to perform daring manoeuvres, once in a while.

Jessamine seized upon the best spell-book, the chief grimoire, the Wizard's prized collection of cantrips. Being as it was such, the book was of mighty size and sumptuous demeanour, its covers sapphire-blue and gilded and its manner self-satisfied. It harrumphed a little as Jessamine leafed through its pages, but it didn't object.

'The trouble is, I hardly know what I'm looking for,' she commented to Tambul.

'Aye,' said he grimly. 'It's not like to be helpfully labelled. "The Queen's Personal Tonic, in Case my Familiar and my Apprentice Should be Obliged to Mix it in My Unexplained Absence" — that'd be nice.'

'You'll get used to it,' offered Jessamine.

'By *it*, I suppose you mean *him*, and I may at that,' grumbled Tambul. 'But not before I lose my wits altogether.'

Jessamine permitted herself a small, smoky snicker. Really, it was invigorating to have someone to grumble with; someone who understood, as she did, how *maddening* the lofty Wizard Garstang could be. Indeed, the Wizard delighted in being so, the wretch; if he had not been threatened with defenestration by a maddened subordinate, he considered the day wasted.

'Oh, but,' she said, arrested in the midst of these pleasant reflections. 'But, Tambul, it *is*.'

'It is what?' Tambul set aside the emerald-bound tome he had been perusing, and Jessamine passed the grimoire down to him.

His face turned thunderous. 'The Queen's Excellent Philtre,' he read aloud. 'For the Information of my Inferiors, Should I be Unable to Oblige Her Majesty.'

The tip of Jessamine's tail began an irritated, staccato twitching.

Tambul's face only darkened further as he read on. 'This is some manner of joke,' he announced. '*One measure of cochineal, ground up fine, dissolved in aqua pura. And let a simple Cantrip be uttered over it, that it might manifest a Starry Radiance.*'

'That doesn't sound too hard,' said Jessamine hopefully.

Tambul shut the book in disgust. 'You really were the worst apprentice, weren't you?'

'Yes,' said Jessamine placidly, having never felt the slightest interest in the mechanics of potion-making. 'So you had better explain the source of your indignation, hadn't you? What's cochineal?'

'*Cochineal, ground up fine*, is the parts of an insect,' he answered. 'Powdered.'

'Some fine, magical insect,' said Jessamine, smiling. 'With healthful properties, for Her Majesty the Queen.'

'A red insect,' said Tambul.

'A powerful, strong colour.'

'No. An insect that is red *only*, with no mystical qualities, Jessamine, not even of any kind. It is a charming colour, I'm told, often used to stain the lips of Court Ladies, and that is all.'

'The… the Cantrip, then?' Jessamine faltered. 'The Starry Radiance—'

'Looks pretty, I grant you, and impressive, if you're disposed to enjoy such things.' Tambul's sour tone left his own feelings on the subject of *sparkles* very clear indeed. 'But of no use to the Queen's health, or anyone's.'

Jessamine turned this information over. 'So we're to mix up a red liquid that looks pretty,' she concluded.

'Yes.'

'And which does nothing at all.'

'Yes.'

Jessamine enjoyed a brief, fervent desire to set fire to the Wizard Garstang's study, but with a strong effort of will, she refrained. 'It isn't a joke,' she offered.

'It must be.'

'It can't be. How could he have known to arrange it? For all his odd talents, clairvoyance was never among them.'

'The whole Library is probably a jest,' muttered Tambul. 'Put here merely to torment us. The *real* Secret Library is somewhere else.'

But Jessamine knew better. She had *one* advantage over Tambul, ignorant as she may be about the potions, and that was seniority. The Library was the real one, and so was the first-favourite-spell-book.

So the Philtre described there must be the one he gave to the queen.

'Was there nothing else written there?' she asked. 'With the measures for the Philtre.'

Tambul scowled, wrenched open the grimoire again, and leafed through it.

'More nonsense,' he said. '*Let it be administered in Her Majesty's Glass-house, at the Golden Hour of the day.*' He shook his head in disgust. 'What possible difference the *place* should make when a Philtre's taken, I can't imagine. And what's the *Golden Hour*?'

'The Golden Hour changes through the year,' said Jessamine. 'Haven't you ever noticed it? It's late after the noon, when the sun sinks low, and all the world is bathed in gold light.'

Tambul's brows rose. 'No,' he said. 'I haven't noticed.'

Tambul clearly possessing the aesthetic sensibilities of a block of wood, Jessamine abandoned all further attempts to enliven his mind. 'The sun's coming up,' she said, uncurling herself from the top of the Wizard's chair, and creeping down. 'We'd better hurry along, if we're to have the stuff by the afternoon.'

'You cannot mean we're to pursue this absurd plan?' Tambul spluttered. 'We're to feed *Her Majesty the Queen* coloured water with stars in it, and call it a Philtre?'

'Yes.'

'But 'tis trickery.'

'If it's trickery, it's the Wizard's trickery,' said Jessamine firmly. 'And once in a while, you know, he has sound reason for the doing of it. To the Mixery, Tambul. We have work to do.'

The Philtre (such as it was) took no time to prepare, Tambul being handy enough at the art. But before that could be managed, there was the cochineal to uncarth (the Wizard not being the organised type, he had left his jar of it, open and half-empty, in the south-facing breakfast parlour). Then a suitable cantrip had to be chosen, for the making of the stars; Wizard Garstang had not seen fit to record his own, preferred charm in the book, and Tambul said, somewhat aggrieved, 'I have not been much in the habit of making things twinkle.'

Jessamine assisted as she could, scurrying hither and thither, and anxiously watched the sun's progress across the sky. More than one carpet, or set of drapes, began to smoke as she passed, and had to be hastily beaten.

At last, though, the mixing was complete, and Tambul declared himself satisfied. He handed a clear bottle filled with carmine liquid to Jessamine, who curled the tip of her tail around the neck of it, and carried it high.

She'd reached the Mixery's stout oak door before she realised he was not following.

'Come along,' said she, giving off sparks.

'My task is to Mix,' he said, rather loftily, gazing down at her from beneath dark brows. ''Tis the Wizard's to administer, or in this case, yours.'

'You think it won't work,' said Jessamine. 'And you'd rather it were my fault, when it fails, and not yours.'

'Of course it will not work. It is coloured water.'

'Will you have a *little* faith in the Wizard, if not in me?'

Tambul's scowl deepened.

'*Something's* bound to happen when the queen drinks your *coloured water*. Do you want to see what it is, or not?'

Tambul heaved a great sigh, and took off his colour-stained apron again. 'Very well.'

'And if it doesn't turn out well, we can always blame the Wizard,' added Jessamine cheerily. 'After all, it's *his* spell-book.'

'That being so—' Tambul agreed, and he swept up the grimoire in question — as proof, no doubt, for when he needed to explain himself to the queen.

The afternoon was speeding by, and the sun was sinking; Jessamine wasted no more time on words, and sped along herself, trusting to the Wizard's apprentice to keep up as he could. The route from the Mixery to the Queen's Glass-house was a winding one, and couldn't be got through quickly.

At length, however, Jessamine burst through the gilded doors and found herself once again embedded in green verdure. The enchanted windows shimmered in the golden light of the dying day, and the place seemed, indeed, different. Warm and mellow and sweet, like bathing in honey.

Queen Mellany sat where Jessamine had left her, in her handsome chair, framed by long-leafed ferns and dreaming lilies. A songbird, feathered in purple and blue, sat on her shoulder, singing.

The queen sat still and slumped, her eyes half closed. But when Jessamine approached, those eyes opened, and fixed upon her. Did they seem a trifle less faded than before, or did the dragon's hopes mislead her?

'Majesty,' panted Jessamine, prostrating herself before royalty — or every part of herself save her tail, which she carried higher than ever. 'We've the Wizard's Philtre for you.'

'But not the Wizard himself.'

'No, Majesty,' Jessamine admitted. 'I haven't seen him.'

'Nor I,' added Tambul, bowing again.

The queen frowned.

'He'll turn up,' Jessamine assured her. 'He always comes back, you know. Like bad weather, or a headache.'

'The Philtre?' answered the queen.

Jessamine swarmed up the arm of the royal throne, and permitted Her Majesty to take the bottle from her. She had to concentrate to keep her sparks and her smokes to herself, and not waft them about; she was a trifle unsettled.

The queen wasted no time, but removed the bottle's stopper at once, and quaffed the starry contents. A smile crossed her weary face immediately — not so *very* dazzling a smile, only a little one, but it was a start.

Then she gave a slow sigh, and settled deeper into her chair.

Jessamine felt a pang of disappointment, having hoped the lady might, with new energy, surge out of her chair, and dance a jig about the glass-house. Or if not quite that, then something equally rewarding.

Tambul's knowing look seemed gloating.

But the queen's posture was losing its *slump*, rather. The smile had not gone away, and her eyes were brighter. She opened them wider, and looked at Jessamine with more interest, and attention, than she had exhibited before.

She scrutinised Tambul, too.

'The Wizard's Minions, is it?' she mused. 'Almost as a good as a whole Wizard, between you.'

'Better,' said Jessamine stoutly. 'For we've not mislaid ourselves.'

'Nor left a whole jar of cochineal out in the open, where anything might have got into it,' said Tambul, less relevantly.

The queen gave a tiny, decorous belch, and out came a star, and floated off. 'He usually stays to talk,' she observed. 'Once I've drunk the Philtre.'

'We could do that,' offered Jessamine. Tambul looked ready to object; she frowned him down. 'What would Your Majesty wish to talk about?'

Queen Mellany considered this, shifting in her chair. It was the first real movement she'd exhibited since the previous eventide. 'Tell me of your day,' she commanded. 'And the making of this Philtre. And the Wizard. Is he good to you? Is he a stern master? I feel that he would be, *quite* stern, but you've such a charming degree of disloyalty towards him I feel I must be wrong.'

'Quite wrong, Your Majesty,' agreed Jessamine, and launched into an account of all that had come to pass; aided, here and there, by Tambul, whose reflections tended towards the sour, but the queen only laughed.

And as the afternoon wore away, and the Golden Hour slowly faded, Jessamine realised that what the Queen needed was less the Philtre and more the friend who brought it.

'You'll come again, will you?' said Her Majesty at last, rising from her chair as the light faded from the skies.

'But of course,' said Jessamine, smiling, and showing all her teeth. 'You'll need another Philtre, won't you? Shall we say tomorrow?'

'The day after,' decided the queen, stretching, and drifting towards the door. 'I shall be quite well until then.'

KNIGHT ERRANTRY

A Wizard in all their glory is a fine sight, as any Court Lady will tell you. They're a peacocking bunch as a rule, fond of their silks and velvets, and like to be lavishly bedecked in jewels. And, after all, why not? To be the *wonder-workers* of the world, the *wielders of cantrip and myth,* the *masters of magic and mystery,* and, above all, the *fixers and mixers of myriad problems (and quaffable solutions)*; this is no insignificant role. Their grateful petitioners are minded to shower them in gratitude; the moveable sort, by preference, composed of *worldly goods* and all that glitters, and why should not they revel in it? The Wizardly arts are not for the faint of heart.

For those of us unused to the splendours of silken mantles and perfumed locks; of rings set with rubies and diamond-studded combs; of embroidered shoes with curling toes, of cloth-of-silver surcoats and tunics gilded in gold, a Wizard in his, or her, natural state, may make an intimidating prospect. Theirs are personalities to match: you'll always know when a

Wizard enters the room. Those smiles are like to be felt on the other side of the Castle, let alone the dining-chamber; they draw attention the way a candle draws moths, and rightly so. A Wizard is *never* ignored.

Formidable, then, a Wizard in public; but what of a Wizard in private?

What, moreover, of a Wizard in *disguise*?

Those flashing colours and shimmering silks serve a sobering purpose, after all. The jungle-cat's patterned hide serves as warning to its prey, so it's sometimes said. A tree-frog's jewel-coloured skin warns away its predators. If you *know* you're in the presence of a Wizard, you know to be on your best behaviour, or at the very least, on your guard.

How much more formidable, then, is a Wizard who's pretending to be somebody else?

And what could he *possibly* mean by it?

To skulk about in disguise is not among the Wizard Garstang's regular habits, to do him justice. His self-satisfaction is of an order that suffers diminishments only begrudgingly. To shed his own, glittering persona; to affect the semblance of some other (and, by definition, lesser) being; this pursuit, be it ever so entertaining, can only grate upon so magnificent a mind.

It could only be undertaken in the case of important business, then. No mere *whim* could separate the Wizard Garstang from his magnificent tunics, or from his enchanted chair. It must be an errand so sacred, so profoundly important, that no one but the Wizard himself could be trusted to undertake it. And yet, an errand that would *not*, in this rare instance, benefit from the open display of all his elegance; not a common occurrence, you might think? Indeed not.

Yet, it happens.

It is known, at the present time, that the Wizard Garstang is not at Castle Chansany (or at least, he does not appear to be). This was discovered by the usual method: when called for, the Wizard did not come, and he kept this up for rather a long time. Long enough to suggest that absent-mindedness, distraction or self-indulgence (the usual culprits) were not the cause of his tardiness, on this occasion. In fact, the Wizard was gone.

Yet nobody saw where he went, not even his faithful Familiar, Jessamine. Subtlety not being a strong suit with the Wizard, this can only have been by design.

He left the Castle by moonlight, as it happens, and alone. By the time his absence was both noted and accepted at Castle Chansany, he was already some miles distant; clad in attire one could only term nondescript and shrouded in a cloak of a plain, unremarkable blue, with the kind of hood whose express purpose is the hiding of the face.

Where was he going?

'To be perfectly honest, madam, I haven't the faintest idea,' said the Wizard Garstang. This question had been put to him by a brisk, sensible sort of woman, not much given to smiling *or* nonsense. He had got as far as the River Ballam by then, and proposed to proceed by boat. The lady and her good husband were ferry-folk, with a small boat between them, and an eye to the Wizard's custom. She had, not unreasonably, asked him where he intended to go.

'We can take you to High Oaks or the Greywater,' said she, unfazed.

'Neither is suggestive of much adventure,' answered the Wizard.

'There's a larger town. Tiven-by-the-Water. But it will take all day to reach it, and it'll cost you dearly.'

The Wizard applied his magnificent mind to the prospect of Tiven Bywater, and was not transported. 'I don't believe that is my destination, either,' he said.

The ferry-woman shrugged, a little disappointed. The Wizard might not have been wearing his jewels, but he had the speech and the bearing of a man of means, and might have made her morning. 'There's naught else within reach of a boat,' said she. 'You've to follow the road down to Balla'dale, then, and try the crossing there. Two days' walk, if you're on foot.' Her glance suggested she had no notion *why* the Wizard was on foot, for he hadn't the look of a man without the means to ride.

She was turning away when the Wizard said: 'No, no. I must go on the water, and it must be here. Your boat seems a splendid craft.' He spoke truly, for these ferry-folk cared for their vessel well. Its hull was clean and sound, its small sail looked in good order, and at the prow rose the carved semblance of a dragon's head. The creature reminded him, passingly, of Jessamine.

'Then choose a destination,' said the woman, patient still, though with an edge to her tone. If the gentleman didn't want her services, there'd be others who would.

'I will know it when we get there. Can you not permit me to board, and simply — go?' He flapped a hand in a down-river direction. 'It's that way.'

He received a narrow look by way of reply, and a long silence.

The Wizard's patience expired. 'I'll pay you five times your usual rate. In fact, here.' He rummaged inside his enveloping cloak, and produced a small pouch. The thing *clinked* as it settled into her outstretched hand.

Not only did it bulge enticingly with coin, but the pouch itself was wrought from a fine-woven fabric most would feel privileged to acquire in a shirt, or perhaps a gown. The ferry-woman's frown vanished in a trice. 'Come aboard,' said she, affable now, and the Wizard settled himself near the dragon-headed prow.

They were not long in departing, for the lady and her husband were true river-folk, happiest afloat. The Wizard turned his face to the wide, silver-lit water, glittering in the rising sun of the morning, and waited.

'Is it that you're looking for something?' asked the ferry-woman's husband, once the business of casting off and setting the sail was completed. He'd taken up an oar and settled into an easy rhythm, slow and steady, for the wind was doing most of the work.

'I am,' answered the Wizard.

'What might that be?'

'I'm uncertain.'

This obscure response befuddled the ferry-man. He fell silent, and remained so, as did his wife. If he'd known he was talking to a Wizard, he wouldn't have given the matter a second thought; Wizards were odd folk, as everyone knew.

An hour passed, and another. The ferry-folk spoke to one another, on occasion — an observation on the wind or the water, a murmured instruction or request. The Wizard didn't speak at all. He sat with his back to those plying the oars, wrapped up to his ears in his heavy blue mantle, and watched the rolling green shores slip by.

What he saw, or sensed, with his Wizard's eyes, no one could have said. He seemed half asleep, dozing the morning away, save that some small sign of tension in his hunched shoulders suggested otherwise, and his eyes were not more than partly closed. He watched for something, and waited, but the morning was gone before it came.

'Hm,' said he, all of a sudden, and sat up straighter. Those keen eyes opened wide at last, and searched the shore intently. They had come to a wooded space by then, grown thickly with fine old trees; possibly the town of High Oaks was near. The ferry-folk looked, and saw nothing of note, not a hint of movement among the green-dappled boughs. But the Wizard's attention was chained.

'Stop!' cried he, some minutes later. 'Stop at once, stop *here*, if you please, I must go ashore.'

This was easier said than done, for the far shore was a distance away, and across a strong current. The ferry-man was heard to utter an oath; his wife maintained a tight-lipped silence.

To do them justice, they tried; pulled hard upon the oars, made what adjustments to the single sail they could. But the river-water carried them far and fast, and the Wizard gave a strangled cry of protest. 'Did I not say *stop?* We are gone too far! Go back! Go back!'

'We cannot go *back*,' growled the ferry-man. 'I

haven't the strength to out-master this current, and neither's my wife. We will set you down when we can.'

The Wizard, impatient, shook his head. He cried out something incomprehensible to the ferry-folk, a few words in a strange tongue none but Wizards understand. And then the true nature of their passenger stood revealed, for what should come soaring over the tumbling river-waters but a *chair*, a very grand chair, with gossamer wings fluttering at all four of its legs. This chair swooped upon the boat, scooped up the Wizard, and sailed away, and that was the last these good ferry-folk ever saw of the Wizard Garstang.

He might, perhaps, have done better to fly from the beginning, save that this errand was to be performed *incognito*, and a flying chair does rather give one's Wizardly nature away. Besides, some stray sense had told him the river was important, and so it had been. He sent the chair upstream a ways, following some direction only he could determine, and when (for some reason) he was satisfied with his location he called, 'Here! Yes, thank you, set me down. Charming. Delightful. Excellent, excellent.' Muttering these various praises, and patting the high back of his favourite chair, he alighted. His boots landed right on the river-bank, the high oaks marching away before him, and he set off without a moment's hesitation, striding away with the water at his back, and his chair bumbling along cheerily behind him.

He seemed to become aware of this well-meaning company only after a few minutes, and turned with some impatience. 'No, that won't do. Cannot you see that I am in disguise? Off with you, my *good* chair, and come back when I call.'

After that he was alone, and seemed at pains to make himself appear harmless. He took down the hood of his mantle, and ruffled up his dark hair (usually so scrupulously ordered, but needs must, after all). He even adopted a pleasant, amiable expression; no easy matter, but he performed the role with admirable dedication until, at last, he came to a halt, and looked about.

He'd stopped beneath an oak-tree much like all the others; high-grown and gnarled, abundant with curled-edged leaves in the freshest green, and sprouting grass-coloured acorns in preparation for the autumn. Below its branches, the forest-floor was earthy and littered with twigs, and had little to recommend it to anyone's particular notice, save for one thing: there lay upon it a bowl.

Earth crusted the bowl so liberally that its precise nature lay hidden. The Wizard noted only that it was large enough to hold a great many of Jessamine's favourite butter-cakes, if she chose to store them there, and it was rather cracked. Shallow, too; more of a basin, perhaps, and so it shall be termed henceforth.

He paused to consider this spectacle, his eyes alight. Two, then three turns around the basin did he take with slow steps, scrutinising the thing from every angle. The basin, as one might expect, did not react — until he bent down, hand outstretched to touch, or perhaps to collect it.

Then it moved. It emitted a thin sound, in fact, like a smothered shriek, and jumped a full four inches away from the Wizard's reaching grasp.

'Oh, come now,' said the Wizard Garstang, crossly. 'I shan't hurt you. In point of fact, I may be able to mend you. Wouldn't you like that? Just look at these cracks! And all this dirt. My Jessamine would be scandalised, and rightly so. She'd have you in the sink and washed-up in a trice, and then you'd gleam like the moon. Hm? Who wouldn't want that?'

The basin seemed unconvinced. When the Wizard tried, again, to sweep it up into his possession, it fluttered and scuttled away, crying piteously. Garstang was obliged to chase it, and he did so, stumbling after, a clumsy gait most unsuited to a Wizard's dignity. This did not improve his temper.

Nonetheless, when he succeeded in laying hands on the fleeing crockery, he did so gently enough. The basin bore its defeat with equanimity, for though it shivered and sobbed, it made no further attempts to escape.

The Wizard applied his sleeve to the encrusted dirt, and wiped some of it away. Underneath, something shimmered golden.

'There, and I thought so,' said the Wizard, incomprehensibly.

When the chair came soaring back, not long after, it took up the Wizard and his new friend both. The basin rode upon the Wizard's lap all the way back to Castle Chansany (there being no further need for subterfuge, now). Garstang clutched it close, his long, agile fingers slowly stroking the basin's rim. His air of amiability was now quite gone; in its place was the light of some anticipation brightening his eyes, and an atmosphere of suppressed excitement.

'A basin,' said Jessamine, upon the following day, when the Wizard was at last to be discovered again where he was supposed to be: in his study. 'You spent days wandering the world — quite without leave or warning, recall — in pursuit of a basin?'

'I did,' said the Wizard gaily, fair frisking about his library. 'A most successful venture.'

'In what fashion, pray?' said the dragon tartly, for she'd had a busy time of it in the Wizard's absence, and was not best pleased.

'Why, *look* at it,' answered her master, and swept an arm (dramatically, flamboyantly, as was his wont) in the direction of the beleaguered basin.

'I am,' said Jessamine, unimpressed. 'A grubby specimen, and broken. Haven't we crockery enough, somewhere about? Could you not have asked the kitchen, if you wanted one?'

'I could have,' agreed the Wizard.

He did not elaborate. Jessamine was not, ordinarily, a slow-witted dragon. It was annoyance that fuddled her wits; but once, with a smoky sigh and a strong effort, she recovered her equanimity, she perceived at once that something must be unusual about this particular basin.

A cursory inspection revealed nothing of the kind, if one discounted the faint glimmer of gold where someone (the Wizard, she concluded from the state of his sleeves) had attempted to polish it. A golden basin, what of that? The Castle was full of such things.

Something else set it apart, then, but perhaps its true nature was beyond the perception of a Familiar. 'It had better be cleaned,' she decided.

'It had indeed. Shall you supervise, Jess-o-mine?'

'If you will.' The sylphs, summoned by some silent request of the Wizards, were already in motion; the basin was swept up by an invisible wind, and borne away to the door. Had it *squeaked* as it rose?

Perhaps it had. Being on excellent terms with the moss-coloured rug, not to mention the best-of-all-chairs and the bookshelves, Jessamine accepted the probability without a qualm.

Even *that* didn't make a basin special, around here.

The basin did not submit quietly to a thorough scrubbing. Jessamine did not so much supervise as stand guard, for the unhappy crockery made several attempts to leap out of the deep stone sink of the Mixery, and make a bid for the door.

The sylphs were brutal, however, and determined, and at last the procedure was complete. The basin stood revealed as glimmering gold from lip to base, and a fine specimen, though no amount of washing could heal the cracks that ran quite through it.

Gold was not prone to developing cracks, thought Jessamine; an oddity, of sorts. And what was so large and valuable a piece of tableware doing out in the depths of the woods at High Oaks, skulking around all by itself?

'There is something fishy about you,' Jessamine informed it.

Once released from the torments of soap and water, and briskly dried, the basin no longer seemed unhappy. In fact, its transformation pleased it, for it stood taller than before, and radiated a smug pride. Its answer to Jessamine's observation was a twinkle she might have been inclined to term roguish, if a basin could be said to possess a capacity for mischief.

'Well, it's better than all that sobbing,' she decided. 'I've to take you back to the Wizard, now. You'll come along peacefully, if you please. I haven't the energy to go chasing through the halls at this hour.'

The basin submitted quietly to being scooped up and swooped away, without so much as a single sob of protest. Jessamine approved of this more cheerful state. Why, at this rate she might even come to *like* the thing.

It was destined for some pride-of-place spot in the Wizard's own lair, she judged, among his many curiosities and rare paraphernalia. That yet another valuable oddity could be worth his sudden departure from the Castle, and a three days' quest to procure it, she still couldn't explain. But Wizards, they had the feathers of peacocks and the hearts of magpies, and one didn't question them if one was wise.

Jessamine wasn't often wise.

'So,' she said, flowing on a wave of smoke back into the Wizard's study. He'd collapsed into the arms of his favourite chair by then, divested of his drab blue mantle, and sat admiring the ruby-red glow of his rings. 'It's a pretty thing, that I'll grant you. But what's so special about it?'

The Wizard beheld the basin's transformation with a vast approval. 'Does the answer yet elude you, my Jess? I am disappointed.'

'And I am growing irascible.' Jessamine breathed a tongue of flame at the Wizard's toes — not quite enough for his velvet slippers to catch on fire, but near.

He laughed. 'Very well, behold. I'll answer this mystery in a moment.'

Jessamine heard these words with a profound scepticism, for the Wizard could be amused by torment. She curled up near the hearth and half-shut her eyes, prepared for a long wait.

She was to be satisfied far sooner than she expected, however, for he sprang out of his chair almost at once, and paced around the basin. It sat in the centre of the moss-coloured carpet, glimmering to itself, and smiling. Perhaps it quavered a little when the Wizard loomed over it, but Jessamine did not think poorly of its courage, for all that. Most people *did* quiver a bit, when the Wizard took it into his head to Loom.

'Well, well,' uttered the Wizard softly, subjecting the basin to a hard stare. Abruptly he sat down on the carpet, cross-legged, and set his chin upon his hand, fingers drumming a rhythm on his own cheek as he thought. 'I *think* I'm correct in my surmise,' he decided after a time. 'But we shall see, shan't we?' He gestured, and a flurry of sparks went up; he cried out a sharp, harsh word in one of his befuddling *other tongues*, and in a waft of blue smoke the basin disappeared.

Jessamine heard a man's voice shouting something, but it was not the Wizard.

When the smoke dissipated, and the study gradually returned into focus, the basin was gone. A man lay sprawled where it had been, inelegantly, as though he had forgotten how his limbs worked. He was dressed head-to-toe in cloth-of-gold; he wore rings and bracelets enough to rival even the Wizard's excesses; and his shoulder-length, reddish hair had been arranged, by someone's careful hand, into a profusion of perfect curls.

In the grip of profound surprise, Jessamine forgot herself so far as to cough embers onto the carpet. 'Forgive me,' she said vaguely, as the carpet writhed and spat to put itself out. She skulked forward on her belly, her tongue unfurled to taste the air near the gold-glittering man.

Royalty.

'You're the prince,' she gasped.

Prince Armael bestowed upon her a dazzling smile. He wasn't handsome, poor soul, as a prince *ought* to be, but with that smile and those clothes he came very near it. 'A dragon!' he announced, in a rich, deep voice. 'I don't recall that we had a dragon before. I'm quite charmed.'

'I'm Jessamine,' she informed him. 'Familiar to the Wizard Garstang.'

'A noble position. I believe I owe my present, immaculate state to your tender ministrations and I thank you.' He spoke cheerfully enough, and he smiled, but his eyes were too wide, and there lay somewhere in the depths of them a wild, hunted look.

'I was his Apprentice before, but I wasn't very good at it,' she observed, babbling. 'Er, your highness? How came you to be a basin?'

A positively enormous question, when it came to it, for the prince had been missing for nigh upon a year. He'd gone out hunting one glorious, autumn morning, and never come home. He had simply gone adventuring, many believed — among them, His Majesty the King. It could have been true.

It *was* true, in fact, for the prince said: 'Do you know, I haven't the faintest idea? I was more than halfway to the sea, last that I recall, and after that—' He shrugged, and embarked upon a lengthy and confused tale, involving a separation from the rest of his party; a thief who'd tried to steal his bow; a chase all the way to High Oaks and beyond; a trading caravan he'd fallen in with thereafter, and kept up with for some time, for no reason he cared to explain; and then an abrupt end came to his recollections, for he'd become a basin, and couldn't recall how it had come about.

'You ran into a Wizard, I shouldn't wonder,' surmised Garstang. 'And made him wroth with you, in some fashion. Or *her*, perhaps. Was there a lady in the case?'

The prince grinned rather sheepishly. 'Perhaps there was,' he allowed. 'Ah well. If so, then she's had her revenge.' He accepted the hand the Wizard offered, and got to his feet. He swayed where he stood for a moment or two, then seemed to gather himself, and turned about.

'I'd better go to Their Majesties,' he decided. 'They'd like to hear what's become of me, I suppose.'

'I imagine they might, at that,' agreed the Wizard. 'Her Majesty in particular, perhaps. She's missed you sorely.'

Prince Armael appeared affected by this news, which raised him in Jessamine's estimation, just a little. 'I'll go at once,' he agreed, and went.

Jessamine considered the Wizard, standing tall, and so pleased with himself. He watched the prince go with a grin of pure self-satisfaction, and then fell into the arms of his favourite chair with a happy sigh. 'Excellent,' he beamed.

'Aye, you'll be peacocking all over the Castle for many a day,' said Jessamine, drifting back to her spot by the hearth. 'Did you know, when you set out, that it was the prince you'd find?'

'Not in the least,' answered Garstang, retrieving a curly glass pipe from some hidden pocket, and lighting it with a flick of his finger.

'Then why did you go? And how did you know *where*?'

'A Wizard learns to pay attention to his Instincts,' said Garstang, with due emphasis on the word.

'I daresay.' Jessamine, disgusted, closed her eyes.

'As does a Familiar,' added Garstang, unexpectedly.

Jessamine's eyes snapped open again. 'Instincts? I'm fair sure I don't possess any.'

'Then you haven't learnt to pay attention.' Garstang puffed a puff of lavender-drifting smoke in her direction, and smiled. 'Take note, Jess-o-mine. Some other day, it could be you hauling an errant prince home to his mother.'

Jessamine favoured the Wizard with an unflattering reflection on the possible nature of his parents. Then, to the sound of the Wizard Garstang's cackle of laughter, she curled her tail over her nose, and went to sleep.

MORE STORIES BY CHARLOTTE E. ENGLISH:

THE WONDER TALES:

Faerie Fruit
Gloaming
Sands and Starlight
Summertide

THE TALES OF AYLFENHAME:

Miss Landon and Aubranael
Miss Ellerby and the Ferryman
Bessie Bell and the Goblin King
Mr. Drake and My Lady Silver

www.charlotteenglish.com